The Hanging of Red Cavanagh

As a young man, Red Cavanagh awoke one morning to find his father dead – murdered by members of the old Willis Walton gang. Setting off in pursuit, he stopped in Bald Hills to secure himself a rifle but didn't succeed. Then, within hours, a grave is discovered in a clearing, covered with a crude wooden cross bearing the name Red Cavanagh. . . .

Four years on and Bald Hills is in deep trouble. The transcontinental railroad is likely to be routed to the north of the town, and a greedy local rancher is seizing property and land aided by gunman Chet Warrener. There seems no hope for the ordinary townspeople.

Until, one day, a stranger rides into town. . . .

The Hanging of Red Cavanagh

Jim Lawless

A Black Horse Western

ROBERT HALE · LONDON

© Jim Lawless 2012
First published in Great Britain 2012

ISBN 978-0-7198-0502-8

Robert Hale Limited
Clerkenwell House
Clerkenwell Green
London EC1R 0HT

www.halebooks.com

Typeset by
Derek Doyle & Associates, Shaw Heath
Printed and bound in Great Britain by
CPI Antony Rowe, Chippenham and Eastbourne

ONE

1855

The gravity of the situation and the grim determination with which he set out to tackle it had put a steely glint into young Red Cavanagh's blue eyes and was causing his jaw muscles to ache. He was grappling with a situation that was beyond his comprehension, contemplating actions that were outside his experience and almost certain to lead to disaster. Yet on that familiar mile-and-a-half ride that took him from the cabin that was his home, along the banks of Lost Creek and into the town of Bald Hills, he knew that there was no alternative.

But even determination and a realization that there was only one course open to him failed to overcome heart-wrenching grief. By the time his sorrel had clattered past Morris Clark's bank, Barney Malone's Blackjack saloon and was turning along Bald Hills' wide main street, his mind was once again in turmoil as he recalled images of the three men he had seen only briefly.

Last night they had ridden in out of the darkness, drawn rein outside the Cavanagh cabin and nodded in a friendly way across the yard to Red as he worked on late-night chores. Once inside the cabin they had talked for a long time to Louis Cavanagh. Some of that talk Red had overheard as he lingered on his way to his room. He had also heard the clink of whiskey glasses, his father's voice raised in anger. Then he had shut the door and climbed into bed. Later, something had wrenched him from a deep sleep and he had left the warmth of his blankets to watch from the window as, in dappled moonlight, the three men had ridden away, taking the same trail into town.

Now, eight hours later and after a night spent tossing restlessly followed by a shocking discovery in the cold light of dawn, Red rode into Bald Hills with the icy realization that he was setting out to hunt down those nocturnal visitors. His intention was to find them, and kill them. He would make them pay with their lives for what they had done to his pa, Louis Cavanagh.

Red had no clear plan in his mind. He was taking it one step at a time, and his first objective was John Vernon's gunsmith's shop. It was midway down the street. Although it was early, there were a few people about. Businessmen were opening their premises. A rider came up the centre of the street, his horse's breath a white mist. Across the street old Denny Coburn, dressed in slack denim pants and a grubby under-shirt, was standing in the wide doorway of his livery barn, which was backed up against a stand of tall pines. Yawning, rubbing his eyes, he saw Red, lifted a hand in greeting – then stared wide-eyed, and jabbed a finger.

Yeah, Red thought. He was seventeen years old, and this was the first time anyone in Bald Hills had seen him wearing a gun. And as he stepped down outside the gunsmith's and tied his sorrel to the rail, he wondered if old Denny realized that what he was seeing hanging loosely from Red's slim waist was Louis Cavanagh's gunbelt carrying the big man's much-used Colt .45.

John Vernon's recognition of the tarnished weapon with its scarred butt was never in doubt.

His dark, deep-set eyes fixed on the gunbelt as soon as the door creaked open and Red walked into his shop. The bone-thin gunsmith leaned forward with his hips against the counter, folded his arms and shook his head reprovingly.

'I don't think I've seen Louis Cavanagh without that Colt strapped about his waist in all the time I've known him. What's your daddy going to say when he goes hunting for it and finds both it and you missing?'

Meticulous as always, Vernon pronounced Cavanagh the correct way, with the emphasis on the middle syllable. Ca*van*agh. Red felt sudden warmth towards a man who had been a friend for as long as he could remember, a twinge of guilt at what he was about to ask.

'I need a rifle, Mr Vernon.'

He felt the gunsmith's keen gaze, lifted a finger to adjust the rake of his grey, flat-crowned hat; nervously played with the plaited rawhide neck-cord hanging in the hollow of his tanned throat.

'You've got yourself your daddy's six-gun, now you want a rifle,' Vernon said musingly. 'You figuring on

7

starting a war, son?'

'I've got cash.'

Red reached into his pocket, pulled out a leather pouch, spilled a jingle of coins on to the counter.

'That something else you took while his back was turned?'

'It's mine. I've been saving.'

'Yeah, and I think the whole town knows why. You and Beth Logan—'

'If all it'll buy is a weapon that's seen some use,' Red cut in, 'that's fine by me. I've got an old Henry, but I need something more reliable, a gun that will home in on any target of my choosing.'

'I gave you that Henry for your tenth birthday, taught you to shoot in the woods behind your cabin. What I'm saying is it's the man, not the gun, puts a bullet where its supposed to be.'

'I'm in a hurry, Mr Vernon.'

'Mind telling me why?'

'Three men rode back through town late last night. You see them?'

'Happens I did. They were strangers, getting on in years – I'd say pushing fifty, and that surprised me. I know the type. Eyes shifting, watching. Hard faces without expression. Hands forever brushing the butt of a six-gun. Not too many of their kind beat the bullet and live on into old age. I saw them ride on through a mite wearily, saw them return to take the same route out of town when the moon was full.'

'Heading south?'

'Looked that way. By now they could be in Nebraska.'

'Those three men killed my pa.'

'They *what*!'

'He's dead,' Red said. 'Lyin' on the living room floor, head all bloody.'

'When did this happen?'

'Last night.'

'And you waited until now—'

'I found him this morning. But that's done, and I'm relying on you to talk to the undertaker, give him a decent burial. What I need now—'

'What you do now is head on down the street and talk to Joe Parody, put this in the hands of the law.'

'Joe's useless, always has been, and this election his time's up. You'll be voted in as town marshal. That's another reason why I'm talking to you, not him.'

John Vernon pursed his lips. His face was troubled. He poked out a finger, absently moved the coins on the counter, shifting them around like pieces on a checkers board.

'Those men. Why'd they kill your daddy?'

'I didn't hear too much.' Red shook his head. 'I know they argued, and he warned them that what they were planning was madness.'

'So he knew them?'

'Sure.'

'Do you?'

'By reputation. You heard of the Willis Walton gang?'

'Dammit, boy, you're not saying—'

'One of those men who rode in was Indian Cole Willis.'

'Indian? They're all white men.'

'Willis moves like one, ghosts around, makes a stalking cat sound noisy. Bad clear through. Another I know for sure was Dustin Walton. The third . . .' Red shrugged, 'I don't know, don't really care that much.'

There was a heavy silence in the little shop that smelled of clean raw timber and gun oil. Vernon's eyes were narrowed and he was drumming his fingers soundlessly on the counter. Red had stepped back a pace. He watched the gunsmith, knew the question that was certain to come next, formulated an answer that would give nothing away. He was also getting ready to run.

'The Willis Walton gang robbed banks, trains, stage coaches over a period of years, then dropped out of sight,' Vernon said softly. 'But there were always four of 'em.' He raised his eyes, looked keenly at Cavanagh. 'What did your daddy have to do with that bad lot?'

'My pa's dead.'

'Yeah, and you want a rifle. You going after those men?'

'When you get around to serving me.'

'A couple of minutes ago I mentioned young Beth Logan. What about her, son? I thought you two were, well. . . ?'

Red felt a sudden lurching sadness. He and Beth Logan had been inseparable since school days, childhood sweethearts who had grown ever closer. Though nothing had been put into words, there was a clear understanding that when both were old enough they would marry, settle down together and raise a family. They saw each other most days. Today was not going to be one of them. Would she understand?

'If you see Beth,' Red said, 'tell her what happened to my pa. Tell her my leaving town has been forced on me by that tragedy, but I'll be gone a few days at most.'

'That's quite a task you're taking on. Apart from the fact they're bad men to go up against, they've got, what, maybe ten hours start?'

'I did say I was in a hurry.'

'I know, but you asking me for a rifle gives me a bad feeling. You're an excellent shot. Sounds like you're planning on picking those men off, one by one, from a distance. For a young lad like you up against men who've robbed and killed, that's probably the safest way of getting even – but shooting from ambush is always cold-blooded murder.'

'Yes or no, Mr Vernon?'

'It has to be no, son. You're biting off way more than you can chew, buying yourself a load of trouble that could ruin your life.'

Mouth tight, Red swept the coins off the counter and was stuffing them into the leather pouch as he turned towards the door. He heard the bang of a wooden flap, knew the gunsmith was coming fast around the counter. Gritting his teeth, he ripped open the door. Run – or deal with the gunsmith? He turned. Vernon was walking quickly, almost on him. Determination was written on his face. Red took half a pace out on to the plank walk. Then he twisted, and swung the heavy pouch high and wide. He put a lot of muscle behind the solid weight. The soft leather packed with metal struck Vernon on the temple. His mouth opened. His eyes glazed. He staggered back, hit the door frame with his shoulder. Then he shook his head. Legs wobbly, he once more came after Red.

But he was too slow. Red was down off the plank walk and swinging into the saddle. The sound of Vernon's yells rang in his ears as he wheeled his horse away from the shop, quickly fading as he spurred the sorrel along Bald Hills' wide main street and headed out of town.

TWO

The marshal's small office was wreathed in cigarette smoke. Joe Parody, greasily bald and almost grotesquely fat, was sitting behind his desk with a battered badge glinting on his vest and a cigarette smouldering under his ragged moustache. His chief deputy, Flatfoot Jones, late forties and in the job for some five years, was standing by the stove warming his bony rear end. Young Tom Clark, over by the window, was the only one of the lawmen not smoking. He was also the only one of the three who'd shown much interest in what John Vernon was reporting.

But that, Vernon knew, was misleading. Parody was interested all right. In the news Vernon had brought, the embattled marshal was certain to see the possibility of strengthening his own position, though that would mean levering his bulk out of his chair and up into the saddle.

'How dead?' Parody said. 'Been plugged, had he? Shot in the back? Because I can't see Louis Cavanagh getting caught cold any other way.'

'Hit over the head, by the looks of it. Flat on his face by the stone fireplace. The room stunk of whiskey – but that was expected, because young Red told me they were drinking.'

'They,' Parody repeated, and then he grinned. 'And you're saying this was the Willis Walton gang?'

'According to Red. He did some listening while they were there, so I'm taking his word for it.'

Parody sucked on his cigarette, dropped it and ground it under his heel.

'They're old men,' he said.

'No older'n me,' Flatfoot said. 'At my age, men are in their prime.'

Parody looked him up and down, and snorted. 'More like over the hill. Anyway, they've not pulled a bank job in Christ knows how many years. They're relics, living on fading memories.'

'But now they could be back,' Vernon said, 'and what you need to find out is what it was they wanted with Louis Cavanagh.'

'How the hell am I supposed to do that,' Parody said, 'with him lying in a pool of blood and his killers long gone? Besides, whatever the hell it was they asked him had nothing to do with Bald Hills. They rode back through town gone midnight. Passed Flatfoot's house, heading south – right?'

The deputy nodded. 'Yeah, I saw them.'

'By now they'll be fifty miles or more away, heading for the Nebraska border.'

'That's pure guesswork,' Vernon said.

'Call it what you like, but all we need to know is

14

they're not here in Bald Hills.'

Flatfoot Jones, tall, lugubrious and as poisonous and slippery as a snake, was shaking his head in disagreement.

'Could be, when he was eavesdropping last night, young Red heard more than he let on to John,' he said, and there was something in the deputy's hooded eyes as he looked sideways at the marshal that aroused John Vernon's suspicions. 'We talk to him, maybe we'll get to the truth, know for sure where those outlaws were heading. Shouldn't be too hard running him down; the boy's been gone no more than a couple of hours.'

Parody was nodding, his moist lips thrust out, his eyes narrowed in thought as he chewed over what the deputy had left unsaid.

'We've only got his word for it that the Willis Walton boys killed his pa,' he said softly. 'Maybe he's right, but either way it'd be a feather in my cap if I brought in Louis Cavanagh's killer, maybe get me enough votes in the coming election to see off my rivals.'

He looked at Vernon and grinned, then began heaving his vast bulk out of his chair.

Thrown off balance by what Parody seemed to be suggesting – Christ, did they really believe Red Cavanagh had killed his pa? – Vernon shook his head in disgust.

'I'm heading over to the undertakers to discuss Cavanagh's funeral. You do what's best, but if you and Flatfoot go after Red, go easy on the lad. And, talking of youngsters, if both of you head out of town that leaves young Tom in charge here.'

'Ain't that cruel of me,' Parody said sarcastically,

15

flashing a glance at the silent, embarrassed young deputy. 'Bald Hills being such a hotbed of crime, I really don't know how he'll cope.'

THREE

Half a mile out of Bald Hills the trail Red Cavanagh was following jinked to the left to run parallel to the western bank of Lost Creek. The terrain was undulating, but not dangerously so, and the nimble sorrel made good time. This early in the day the sun was not yet hot enough to dissipate the thin early morning mist. The air was fresh, the high peaks of the Wind River Range to the north west were lost in the clouds. To the south the land was mostly flat and green all the way to the Nebraska border.

Unlike Marshal Joe Parody, Cavanagh had no preconceived notions on which direction the three Willis Walton men had taken. Instead, thankful for the rain that had fallen heavily over the past few days, softening the earth, he was relying on tracking skills honed by hunting elk and bear on frequent trips with his father to the thick forests of the Wind River Range foothills.

First, leaning out of the saddle as he rode, he identified the tracks left by the three men's horses, separating them from others both old and new. Then, with their characteristics fixed in his mind – one horse had a worn left hind shoe, another had thrown a couple of nails, a third appeared to be carrying a man of considerable weight – he was able to relax a little and give some attention to what might be going on behind him.

He didn't expect the sounds of a posse to reach him any too soon. Vernon had listened to his story and would pass it on, but it was unlikely Joe Parody would consider it worthwhile going after the Willis Walton gang. The three men had done nothing in the town to justify a pursuit and, to anyone riding up to the cabin, the way Louis Cavanagh had died would look more like an accident than cold-blooded murder. Besides, Red's scathing assessment of the fat marshal's usefulness in John Vernon's shop had been on the nail: Parody was lazy, rarely moved out of his office, and when the elections were held he was certain to be replaced by Vernon.

The idea that Joe Parody would be considering another, easier option – prodded into that way of thinking by Flatfoot Jones who knew he'd also be out of a job if the marshal was replaced – never even occurred to Red Cavanagh.

It was late summer in Wyoming, and before too much time had passed the sun had become uncomfortably hot. The areas of woodland Red rode through offered some relief, the overhead canopy of green leaves transforming the direct glare into pleasant dappled shade while the damp emanating from the undergrowth cooled the air. He followed the horses' tracks for almost an hour. Once or twice he lost them as the shallow marks became too difficult to read on harder ground. Riding in a widening circle with his eyes to the ground had enabled him quickly to locate them again, and he had not been seriously troubled.

Then, as he rode from hot sunlight into another cooling stretch of sparse woodland, the trail cut through the centre of a small clearing and the tracks swung sharp left.

Red took the turn, eased the sorrel back to a slow walk and dragged a sleeve across his damp forehead. Then, eyes searching the ground for sign, he did a slow circuit of that side of the clearing. He saw the remains of a camp-fire. Close to it, but up against the trees, he saw crushed grass and depressions in the ground that indicated where the three men had dumped their saddles, rolled their blankets and slept.

But only for a couple of hours.

Once again he picked up the tracks left by the three horses. These were much fresher. If the ones that led off the trail into the clearing had been made some time after midnight last night, these had been made in the early hours of the morning: the men had slept briefly, breakfasted hurriedly, then resumed their journey.

It was the way that journey had been continued that was causing Red Cavanagh to tip back his Stetson and scratch his head.

Instead of swinging out on to the trail and turning again to the south to resume their journey, the three men had ridden to the inner edge of the clearing, down a gentle slope through the trees and straight into the shallow waters of Lost Creek. The evidence was clear: their horses' hoofs had left deep impressions in mud and gravel.

Why had they done that? There was no trail leading south along the creek's eastern bank. The land became progressively rougher and overgrown, reaching a state were it was virtually impassable to a man on horseback.

To the north, Red knew, conditions were much more favourable. Indeed, as a rider approached Bald Hills the going became much easier. That led to just one conclusion: the Willis Walton men had crossed the creek and headed back towards the town.

Which left Red with the same intriguing question: Why?

Red was pondering on this, the question still unanswered but with some uneasy suspicions forming, when the crack of a shot snapped him back to reality with a jerk. He heard the sharp report, the hum of the bullet – and realized with disbelief that he was the target. A second shot rang out. He gasped as what felt like a red-hot iron raked across his ribs. Skin prickling with shock, he spun his sorrel and spurred it into the woods.

He took the frightened animal in hard, smashing and crackling through undergrowth, then tumbled from the saddle. The horse snorted and trotted away, eyes wild. Red hugged the moist, leafy ground; wriggled forward; rolled behind the trunk of a tall tree. There was now solid timber between himself and the gunman. Hot lead from the next volley chipped green splinters from the trees, or howled harmlessly into the blue skies.

Who was trying to kill him? Where where they?

Swiftly, Red picked up the faint drift of smoke that revealed the gunman's position on the opposite side of the clearing. Keeping down, he drew big Louis

Cavanagh's six-gun and blasted several fast shots in a hail of return fire.

The clearing was no more than thirty yards across. The gunman was using a rifle. At that range a rifle's efficiency was reduced. It became unwieldy. A good man with a handgun had the advantage. Proof of that was a sudden yelp of anger, or pain. Red's shots were getting uncomfortably close, had maybe drawn blood. Encouraged, he fired until the hammer clicked on an empty chamber, then rolled on to his back. Fingers shaking, he pressed shells from his father's gunbelt and reloaded.

That done, ears alert to danger, he laid a hand on his ribs and pressed gingerly. The pain was raw, brought tears to his eyes. His hand came away sticky, but there was not the grating feel of a broken rib. Fumbling, he stripped off his bandanna, folded it into a thick pad and stuffed it under his shirt.

Then, gritting his teeth, he rolled over again and sent three fast shots across the clearing.

The response was unexpected.

'Stop that damn shooting,' a voice cried. 'This is the law, and you're under arrest.'

Joe Parody, Bald Hills' marshal. What the hell was going on?

Red Cavanagh sat up, planted his back hard against the tree trunk, felt his pulse hammering.

'Joe, this is Red,' he called breathlessly.

'I know who it is.'

'If you knew it was me here, why did you start shooting?'

'That's not the way it was. You rode straight at me, shot to kill. You were resisting arrest. Put down your gun, kid. I'm taking you into town. The charge is murder.'

Red's laugh was hollow.

'Your second shot got me across the ribs. I'm bleeding like a stuck pig.'

'Forget it. Worse is coming. You murdered your pa, smashed his head with a fire iron. For that, you'll hang.'

'John Vernon was going up to the cabin. That's not the story he would have brought back.'

'Vernon's a gunsmith, with no authority. It was my job as town marshal to investigate a reported killing. It was me went up there, and I know what I saw.'

Red's breathing was easing, his pulse slowing. He knew Parody was lying. Authority or not, John Vernon would not have allowed the no-good marshal to ride up to the cabin on his own. And the story Parody was telling was pure concoction. Louis Cavanagh was dead, but he had not been clubbed with a fire iron.

'I didn't kill him.'

'That's what I'd expect you to say. But right now I'm giving you sixty seconds to put your gun down and walk out here clutching handfuls of sky.'

The sun filtering through the trees was hot on Red's face. He could feel the salt sweat drying stiffly. His bloody wound was sticking to the padded bandanna. Easing his position against the tree, he wriggled down painfully so that he was again facing the clearing. He lifted his six-gun.

Parody's game was clear. The man was fighting to

hold on to his job. What better way to do it than to lead a successful hunt for a killer? Trouble was, the lies he was telling might not hold up in court. He'd be aware of that, so likely he wouldn't be planning on taking Red back to town. His first idea would have been to let Red run, then gun him down. His second. . . ?

Dammit, Red thought, he said I'd hang. Was that the man's intention? To string him up from the nearest tree?

With his life at stake, Red knew he dare not wait for the full sixty seconds to pass – and half a minute had already slipped away. Lifting his head, he squinted across the clearing. It was possible Parody had changed his position, but the man was no tactician. He'd spent too long sitting in his office chair.

Allowing himself a thin smile, Red thumbed back the hammer and drilled fast shots in a line across the bushes where he had seen drifting gunsmoke.

There was no response. No answering shots. No cries of anger. No fresh orders to put down his gun.

Instead, from behind him, there came the oily click of a shell sliding into a rifle's breech.

'It's all over, kid.'

Red rolled clumsily away from the tree. Pain ripped across his ribs. His right arm was trapped beneath his body. He was agonisingly slow shifting his weight. When he wrenched his arm free and brought his six-gun to bear he knew, with a feeling of utter despair, that it was too late.

Flatfoot Jones was sitting languorously in the saddle. In one hand he held two sets of reins, his own, and

Red's sorrel's. In his other hand he held a Winchester rifle. The muzzle was lined up on Red's chest, and the lanky deputy's forefinger was white on the trigger.

'He was my father,' Red Cavanagh said. 'After my mother died that man looked after me the whole of my life.'

'Except when he was away for weeks on end,' Parody said. 'We always did wonder where the hell he went, you a mere pup, fending for yourself. Well, now we know. The Willis Walton boys, there was always four of 'em. Seems your daddy had a secret life outside Bald Hills.'

'Why would I kill him?'

'Should be me asking you that question. Don't know why I didn't think of it.'

Parody winked across at Flatfoot Jones. The deputy was mounted, and had worked his horse up alongside Cavanagh's sorrel. His hand was clamped on the sorrel's bridle, hard up against the bit, forcing the nervous animal to remain stock still. His other hand was slack at his side. From it dangled a cocked six-gun.

Red Cavanagh's hands were tied behind his back. He was sitting stiffly upright in the saddle. There was a noose around his neck. The big knot was bunched against the bone behind his ear. The rope from which the noose was fashioned had been thrown over the strong branch of a tall tree, the loose end allowed to fall, then tied to the trunk. Before being secured, the rope had been pulled taut.

'I didn't kill him,' Red said. His thoughts were wild, out of control, his throat dry, the stiff rope of the noose

24

like an iron bar above his Adam's apple. 'John Vernon will know I'm innocent. You'll never justify what ... what you're about to do. It's a lynching, it's—'

'You resisted arrest,' Parody said mildly, and he reached up to touch the red bloodstain where one of Red's bullets had grazed his shoulder. 'When overpowered, you confessed. With commendable courage, you asked me not to take you back to town in disgrace.'

'Jesus Christ, you lying sonofabitch,' Red said hoarsely. He gasped, tried to ease his neck in the noose, squinted at the tall deputy and said, 'You can stop this. Are you going to let him drag you down with him?'

'I obey orders,' Flatfoot Jones said.

'Yeah, well, that'd be a first,' Parody said drily. 'I hate to tell you this, kid, but that skinny fellow holding your horse gave me the idea. Said there was no doubt about your guilt, so why not get it over. Told me with an election coming up, I need all the help I can—'

He broke off. The muted drumming in the background that had gone unnoticed behind the drone of insects and the torrent of lies had suddenly swelled into the thunderous beat of hoofs. Three riders came hammering down the trail from Bald Hills and swung into the clearing. They drew rein in a shower of dirt and stones, dismounted in a skilful continuation of that manoeuvre and only then noticed that they had company.

One, the taller of the three, took in the situation at a glance.

'What the hell?' he said softly. With his hand reaching for his six-gun, he began walking towards Flatfoot Jones.

Red had his head twisted around to see what was going on. He had no trouble recognizing the men, for it was the second time he'd seen them in the space of twelve hours. Suddenly his heart was pounding. The raw wound across his ribs, the rope around his neck – everything was forgotten as hope flared.

Jones had gone white. He whipped his hand away from the sorrel's bridle. Panicking, he began turning his horse. Forgetting that the six-gun in his hand was cocked, his sudden movement caused him to tighten his grip. His forefinger squeezed the trigger. The crack of the shot was deafening in the clearing's hot silence.

As it rang out, sending black birds flapping skywards, the sorrel took off. It reared, forelegs flailing. For an instant the pressure on Red's neck was relieved. Then the thrashing forelegs came down and from a standing start the horse bounded straight into a hard gallop that would take it across the clearing towards Lost Creek. Red Cavanagh felt the saddle whipped away from beneath him. The cantle hit him hard at the base of his spine. Then he dropped straight down. The rope was tight, so there was no distance for him to fall. But that made it worse. Instead of being stunned as the hard knot hit him behind the ear, he finished up twirling lazily at the end of the rope. The noose was up under his chin. All his weight was pulling downwards. The knot's position forced his head forwards. Very slowly, he began to strangle.

FOUR

'I'm truly sorry for your loss.'

John Vernon was sitting behind Joe Parody's desk. There was a badge pinned to his vest. His words had been directed at the dignified man in the dark suit and white shirt with stiff collar. Morris Clark was the owner of Bald Hills' bank. He was sitting on a hard chair, the sun at his back. He was numb with grief.

'He was doing his job,' he said. 'Those three men. . . .'

He trailed off, swallowed, shook his head.

'The Willis Walton gang,' Vernon said. 'I know they left town last night, because I saw them go. Maybe someone else did, too, but that was their intention. They wanted to be seen, wanted us to think they were miles away from Bald Hills, to hell and gone. But what they must have done was spend the night just a few miles to the south, then set off this morning and circle around, come back into town from the north. That way, the first building they'd come across is your bank. It was well planned – like all their jobs. They were in and out in minutes.'

'And Tom?'

'It was pure chance that Tom was up that end of town.'

'And chance became bad luck.'

'Yes. I suppose he wondered why there was a mounted man outside the bank, holding two horses. Questioned him, maybe got a a grin, a vague answer. So he loosened his gun and went inside to find out what was going on.' Vernon spread his hands. 'You were there, Morris, you'd heard the shouting, you were coming out of your office. You saw it happen. Men like that, outlaws, they don't wait to ask questions. Besides, Tom had a badge pinned to his vest. He was gunned down as soon as he walked in the door.'

'There is a saying commonly used in situations such as this,' Morris Clark said, shaking his head despairingly, 'and it's all to do with life going on. It does, of course, and I'm not the only man to be anticipating a deal of suffering. Money was taken from my bank. I don't even know if I can continue in business. But I can say with absolute certainty that while I'm poring over figures with the man who does my accounts and hoping to find a way out of this mess, big businessmen are going to be left short. One is the Slash L owner, Grant Logan. Bad enough, of course, but he's a strong man and should be able to cope.' He hesitated. 'I don't know if I can say the same for you, Alan.'

Alan Forsyth laughed softly, and shook his head. He was tall and grey, with warm brown eyes but a face so deeply lined it appeared scarred. He'd been standing looking out of the window, but turned to face the room at Clark's words.

'D'you think I've been too badly affected by my troubles, Morris? Well, losing my wife knocked one leg out from under me, and Ellie coming off her horse and ending up walking with a stick just about put paid to the other.' He lifted his head, his gaze steady. 'But the A Bar F won't run itself, with or without money.'

'Point taken, Alan,' Clark said, 'and you're right, of course. As the biggest rancher north of town you're better placed than most to weather the storm. As for Ellie, well, John knows her better than just about anybody. . . .'

'John Vernon,' Forsyth said firmly, 'has done more than anyone to get Ellie through her troubles. It brought them closer, if that was possible – and I want you to know, Morris, that now trouble's come knocking on your door, well, we're all there if you need us.'

There was silence for a moment. Then the burly man standing silently near the gun cabinet cleared his throat.

'Tom Clark had the makings of a fine deputy, but it was wrong for Parody to leave him on his own.'

'Of course it was,' Vernon said. 'But Parody's job was on the line, and he was in a hurry. He had nothing on the Willis Walton boys, believed they were long gone and chasing them would be a waste of time. He took Flatfoot with him and went after Red Cavanagh. At the time my mind had other priorities, so I wasn't paying too much attention. It was only later that I became convinced Parody was after glory; he was set on pinning the death of Louis Cavanagh on his son, Red.'

The burly man was grey-haired, distinguished while

retaining the blunt, rough-hewn way of the Wyoming countryman. His name was Lewis Edgar. He was head of the Bald Hills' town council, and despised Joe Parody.

'What about you, John? As Bald Hills' new marshal,' he said, 'what's your opinion?'

'I reckon Joe Parody will blow his top,' Vernon said, deliberately choosing to misunderstand the question. The quick grin that followed held no humour. 'If you mean what do I think about Louis Cavanagh's death, well, first off, Red reckons the Willis Walton boys killed him. He's basing that on the argument he overheard. Me, I'd go for accident: looked to me like the man had drunk so much whiskey he was out on his feet, fell down and banged his head on the stone fireplace.'

'Wouldn't Red have to be pretty certain in his mind it was a killing to walk in on you demanding a rifle, then set off after those three outlaws?'

'If Joe does bring him in, he'll be accusing the boy of murder. What Red has to say in his defence will go some way towards answering your question.'

'But you believe he's innocent?'

'Without any doubt whatsoever.'

'Well, they're here now,' Edgar said, glancing towards the window. 'Parody and Jones – but they don't have Red with them.'

Dust and hot sunlight flooded into the room as Edgar flung open the door. Parody and Jones had tied up at the rail. Their boots hammered on the boards as they crossed the plank walk. Edgar stepped away and the fat man barged past him into the room. Flatfoot Jones followed. They brought with them the smell of horses and raw sweat. Vernon was aware of something indefinable in their manner that suggested defeat, and something else. Guilt? Realization that they'd made a foolish decision? Had they already heard the news of the robbery as they rode into town?

Joe Parody saw Vernon, his position behind the desk, the gleaming badge, and understood the situation at a glance. His face turned ugly.

'Give a man a goddamn inch,' he said savagely, and flung his stained Stetson at a peg. Then he looked from Vernon to Lewis Edgar, and finally noticed the bank manager, Morris Clark.

'What's going on? Where's Tom? And how come I get replaced in my absence, when every damn one of you knows I stood a good chance of winning the election?'

'Leaving town was a bad mistake. It's the last one you'll make as marshal,' Lewis Edgar said. 'Jones can keep his badge; I'll give him the benefit of the doubt and assume he was following your orders. As for Tom, your young deputy's dead. He was gunned down in cold blood when, in your absence, the Willis Walton gang robbed Morris Clark's bank.'

Parody's eyes widened. Pulling across a flimsy chair, he dropped heavily into it, causing it to creak in protest. He dragged a hand across his red face, looked across at Flatfoot.

'That's not all they've done,' Flatfoot Jones said, as if on cue. 'Last night they murdered Louis Cavanagh. Today they caught up with Red, strung him up.'

'We came across them by chance, rode straight into

31

trouble,' Parody said in a voice dripping with regret. 'Because of the way it happened, I put myself partly to blame for Red's death.'

John Vernon listened with scepticism he could not hide. Parody had dragged his chair across to the side of the desk that had once been his, and placed it so he could look at everyone in the room simply by moving his eyes. Sweat was pouring down his face. He held a dirty handkerchief in his fat fist, and kept mopping his forehead, his cheeks.

'So how did it happen?' Vernon said.

'We surprised them, disturbed a neck-tie party,' Parody said. 'Hell, we thought they were miles away. We rode into a clearing ten miles south of town – you know it well – pulled off the trail for a smoke and suddenly we're mixed up in a lynch mob: three men, with young Red up on his horse with his hands tied and a noose around his neck.'

'They started shooting as soon as they saw us,' Flatfoot Jones offered from the window. 'All three of 'em. Well, that meant one thing, didn't it?'

'The man holding Red's horse let go and went for his six-gun,' Parody said, 'that's what it meant. Soon's the shooting started, that sorrel took off like a frightened deer. Went out from under Red, and the kid was left swinging at the end of the rope.' Theatrically, he mopped his face again, paying particular attention to his moist eyes. 'Damn it,' he said, putting a catch in his voice, 'if we hadn't rode into that clearing there'd've been no shooting, and if the shooting hadn't started—'

'Red would have died anyway,' Lewis Edgar said

bluntly. 'He was on his horse, the rope around his neck. What the hell do you think those men were going to do to him?'

'Nevertheless—'

'Edgar's right,' Vernon said, 'so why don't you stop play-acting? If you'd had your way, Red would have ended up back here facing a murder charge. If convicted, he'd have gone to the gallows. Looked at that way, those outlaws saved you a heap of trouble.'

'Hell, that's not—'

'What I'd like to know,' Vernon cut in, 'is how those men robbed the bank here in Bald Hills, but still managed to get to that clearing ahead of you.'

'I was following tracks, playing Indian,' Flatfoot Jones said quickly as Parody's mouth flapped soundlessly. 'They got a mite confusing and we lost a lot of time. I guess those outlaws rode on by when we were deep in the woods.'

Edgar uttered a sharp exclamation. Vernon shook his head in disgust.

'So later, when you blundered on them and they opened fire,' he said, 'What did you do?'

'Got the hell out of there,' Joe Parody said.

'Without returning fire, fighting back, trying to save Red?'

'I was wounded in that first volley,' Parody said, and he clutched at his ripped shirt, turned so they could see the dried blood. 'The kid was dead, his neck broke. My only thoughts were for the living – my deputy, Jones – and to get back here fast and raise a posse.'

'There'll be no posse,' Vernon said. 'This is a small

town. I'm not going to take hard-working men away from their livelihood. Any pursuit of the Willis Walton gang could drag on for days, weeks.'

'I agree,' Lewis Edgar said, rising from his chair. 'However, a small party must ride out to recover Cavanagh's body. I think you should do that, John. Leave Jones here. Take Parody with you if he's that keen to make amends.'

'I'll go along,' Clark said.

Edgar frowned. 'You've got a bank to run, Morris. If those outlaws are hanging about you could be riding into trouble.'

Clark was on his feet.

'I hope they are. After what happened to my boy, sitting in my office would be pure torture. Helping bring Red's body back to town will assuage some of that grief. The possibility that I may be able to exact some kind of revenge has me raring to go – and John Vernon knows that I'm an excellent shot.'

FIVE

In one of the rooms behind the jail office, Joe Parody swapped his ripped and bloodstained shirt for a clean one. Morris Clark walked to his home on the western outskirts of the town and changed from his business suit into worn clothes more suitable for a strenuous ride in the afternoon heat. He also strapped on his six-gun.

John Vernon was wearing denims and a cotton shirt under a leather vest. He walked back up the street to his shop and returned carrying the weapon that Red Cavanagh had been denied: a Winchester repeating rifle. And Vernon couldn't help wondering, with a deep feeling of regret, if that weapon would have helped save the kid's life.

Without stating the gruesome reason, Joe Parody suggested taking a buckboard with them. Vernon opted for a spare horse. A dead man, he reasoned, would not notice the discomfort of being tied belly down. He crossed the street to the livery barn with Clark when the banker went to collect his horse. The old hostler, Denny Coburn, sucked his gums, listened attentively with narrowed, rheumy eyes, then willingly handed over a tough looking mustang and a lead rope.

Ten minutes later, with the lanky figure of Flatfoot Jones watching from the plank walk, they rode out of Bald Hills.

This time there was no need to follow tracks. With the hot sun beating down on them, its rays sometimes filtering through tall trees but mostly hitting them direct, they rode at a fast lick along the trail following the course of Lost Creek. Possibly forgetting that he was no longer in charge, no longer the marshal of Bald Hills, Joe Parody took the lead. He rode his usual pony that was understandably sway-backed. The big man rode with his legs stuck out at an angle, his fat body bouncing cruelly as the small horse cantered down the trail. Vernon could see the sweat glistening on the lardy flesh of Parody's neck, could hear the horse snorting as it valiantly tried to keep its legs from buckling under the weight of the man grunting at the discomfort of the hard saddle.

Vernon rode some yards back, the narrow trail often forcing him stirrup-to-stirrup with Morris Clark. Few words were exchanged. Vernon's thoughts were with Red Cavanagh, the rifle that was now tucked into the worn leather boot under his thigh and what it might have done for the kid. Clark was fighting grief, and no doubt hoping that he would come face to face with his son's killers. And, yes, he would be thinking in the plural. Clark had been in the bank, had watched his son die. One man had pulled the trigger but in the father's mind, and in the eyes of the law, all three of the bank robbers were equally guilty.

It was some ten miles to the clearing. They made it in less than an hour. Half-dozing in the saddle, Vernon was taken by surprise when Joe Parody suddenly hauled his pony over to the left. They rode out of the trees on to baking hot, hard-packed earth, which had all moisture sucked out of it by the sun. Eyes everywhere, Vernon saw the impression of hoofs made by horses ridden hard into the clearing when the earth was night-damp, the remains of the fire where the Willis Walton gang had camped for what had remained of the night. He watched Parody cut away to the right, ride up to the trees marking the perimeter of the clearing and pull to a sudden halt.

'Nothing there,' he called. 'Red's gone. The rope's gone.'

'You sure you've got the right place?'

Vernon rode over, ignored Parody's angry stare then looked up as the ex-marshal pointed to the horizontal branch. It was scarred where Red's weight swinging on the end of the rope had caused it to cut into the bark.

'Lynch mobs leave bodies hanging as a deterrent,' Parody said. 'Ain't never known a mob to cut a victim down, then give him a decent burial.'

'There was nobody to deter, no reason for a dead young man to be left to scream a warning. This whole affair sounds like some kind of revenge attack on the Cavanagh family, pure and simple.'

'Still makes no sense. Bank robbers, taking time to bury a man.'

37

'You don't know they've done that.'

But Parody was not listening. Instead his eyes were searching, and now he pointed vaguely and slid down from the exhausted pony. He lumbered away into the trees, a bull of a man, somehow finding a path through the crackling undergrowth. When Vernon joined him, the fat man was standing with hands on hips looking down at the mound of fresh earth he'd spotted. He was frowning. His lips were moving as he read the words on the crude cross. It had been fashioned from a split log, the cross-piece tied with rawhide, the whole then hammered into the ground at the grave's head.

'*Red Cavanagh*,' he said. '*Age 17 years.* Burned into the wood with a red-hot iron.'

'Well I'll be damned,' John Vernon said softly.

'They hanged him, then buried him,' Parody said. 'That just don't make any kind of—'

A shot rang out. Joe Parody grunted once, then collapsed in a heap. Vernon gazed, horrified, at the black hole in the centre of the marshal's forehead, the trickle of dark blood. Dropping swiftly to one knee, his eyes wildly probed the trees. Parody had been facing into the woods. The shot had come from a roughly southerly direction. Even as the crude calculation was made, he received confirmation.

'One man, John,' Morris Clark called. 'In front, over to your left a ways.'

'Get down,' Vernon yelled. 'Take cover.'

The banker had stayed with the horses, not moved into the trees. From his position out in the open he had a wide field of view, but he was also perilously exposed.

The gunsmith in Vernon told him the man Clark had spotted was using a rifle. To put a slug between Parody's eyes he had to be an excellent shot. Now it seemed that he was staying back out of six-gun range. He had chosen his position well. From cover he could wait for a careless movement, kill again with a well-aimed second shot.

Those registered thoughts screamed a warning to Vernon: to remain where he was would be suicidal. He sucked in a deep breath of hot air. Then, tearing his dis-believing gaze from the big man lying dead at his feet, he came up off his knees in a rush and turned to run. Thorns immediately ripped at his shirt, almost dragged him off his feet. As he staggered sideways the second shot cracked. It was as if a hot needle had pierced his ear. A hot trickle of blood wormed its way down his neck.

His rifle was with his horse. The frightened animal was no more than twenty yards away, quivering, but for now held still by the trailing reins. Feeling the skin on his back crawling, Vernon thrashed towards it through the undergrowth. Clark had moved away from the horses, looking for a clear shot. Vernon heard him open up with his six-gun. There was an answering crack from the hidden rifle. The bullet snicked a twig close to Vernon. The gunman was ignoring Clark, going for the closer target, hampered by the thick undergrowth.

Almost blinded by salt sweat trickling into his eyes, Vernon knew panic was slowing him down. He was so close to the edge of the trees he could imagine reaching out to touch his horse. But somehow he had strayed from the path Joe Parody had found on his way to the grave. He was deep in thick scrub. By wildly fighting the clinging branches and sharp thorns, he was becoming ever more entangled.

Cursing softly, he stopped, stood still. He turned. Dropping to a half-crouch, knowing his life now depended on it, he drew his six-gun. With his other gloved hand he began to rip aside the restraining fronds, tearing thorns from cloth. He paused in his efforts to drag a sleeve across his eyes, clear his vision. Resuming, he searched the woods for a target. There was a sound away to his left. Was there a shadow moving through dappled sunlight?

Uncertain, Vernon snapped a shot, then another. The hairs on the nape of his neck prickled as a man laughed softly – away to his right.

Jaw clamped, Vernon knew he'd fallen for an old trick. There was no moving shadow. A stone had been thrown. The movement had been nothing more than the soft breeze whispering through high, thin branches. As he turned, lifted his six-gun, he had the sick feeling of dread in his stomach that told him he was too slow, too late.

Then the rifle cracked, sang its deadly song, and John Vernon's right leg was hit by a violent blow between knee and ankle. He heard the dull snap of bone breaking inside torn flesh. Suddenly he was a one-legged man with nothing to grasp, nothing to hold on to. He went down in the scrub with a tearing crackle, lay on his back looking up at the sun and waited for the shot that would kill him.

There was a sudden rush of sound, of heavy breathing. Vernon blinked, flung an arm across his eyes as he was showered with falling leaves and twigs. A man leaped over him, moving *into* the woods. Then there was a single crack from the rifle. It was answered by a fierce volley of shots. A man cried out. The sound was choked off, wetly. It was a muted, dying gurgle. The silence that followed was the hush of mourners at the side of a grave. The hot air reeked of cordite, of sap from torn branches, of the sour sweat of anger and of fear.

A shadow fell over Vernon.

'It's over, John,' Morris Clark said. His face was animated as he dropped to one knee by the downed marshal. For the moment, the grief that had been so evident in his voice had been banished by triumph fuelled by an intense adrenalin rush. In the hand he used every day to dip a pen into ink and write laboriously in bank ledgers he was holding a smoking six-gun. It looked as if it belonged there.

'It is for me,' Vernon said shakily. 'All over. My leg's gone, that bullet snapped the bone.'

'Doc Liberson's a worker of miracles.'

'There's two dead men out there, Morris—'

He broke off as pain hit him, ripping through his leg like a hot knife, from ankle to deep in his groin.

'If you think I'm dragging rocks and brushwood in this heat to keep animals from chewing up those sons of bitches,' Clark said, 'then think again. Come on, John. Let's see if we can get you up on your horse and back to town before you bleed your life away.'

John Vernon was thinking of that one-sided conversation three weeks later, and feeling pretty pleased with himself. Despite the agony of the broken leg, once he got back to Bald Hills with Morris Clark and two spare horses he'd made damn sure a party rode back down the trail. They had orders to bury Joe Parody and the dead member of the Willis Walton gang.

Lying on his settee with his plastered leg stretched out stiffly, he was also quietly amused. He'd been town marshal for just that one day; hell, not even that. Must have been less than eight hours between Lewis Edgar pinning the badge on his vest and that same man taking one look at the damage done to Vernon's leg and relieving him of his post.

Shortest on record, Vernon mused. And he'd handed over to Flatfoot Jones, named because of his big, splayed feet. Not young, not the straightest of men in the moral sense, but nobody could deny his experience. Edgar had sworn him in, albeit with a measure of reluctance.

It was Marshal Flatfoot Jones who at that moment knocked on John Vernon's door and walked into the room above the gunsmith's shop.

He was carrying a newspaper.

'We were wrong about Louis Cavanagh,' he said.

'What, he's still alive?'

Jones blinked. 'No. Can't be. We buried him.'

Vernon sighed. 'Yes, I know we did. So tell me, in what way were we wrong?'

'Louis had nothing to do with the Willis Walton gang. He wasn't the fourth man.'

'Did you think he was?'

'Joe did. He was convinced.' He flapped the paper. 'What those outlaws did, they hanged Red, buried him—'

'Took his horse.'

Flatfoot nodded impatiently. 'Did that, yes, then rode across open country to Nebraska Territory and made for Boulder City. Must have met up with the fourth man there – only now he was the third man, because the original third man was plugged by Morris Clark after he ruined your leg.'

'That was Dustin Walton; you had an old Wanted dodger made that clear,' Vernon said. 'OK, and then what? They robbed the bank in Boulder City?'

'Damn right they did. And another of 'em died there, gunned down as he climbed on his horse. Somebody had cut his cinch. Put his foot in the stirrup, the saddle came down, damn near fell on top of him. He was plugged as he lay there, by a man owns a general store in Boulder and is now a hero.'

'Two left,' Vernon said thoughtfully, and he poked a stick inside his cast and scratched an itch on his shin.

Flatfoot grinned. 'Guess they made a mistake returning to their wicked ways after so long away.'

'That they did,' Vernon agreed. 'But one thing puzzles me. Why the hell did they ride up to Louis Cavanagh's cabin in the middle of the night and spend three hours talking?'

SIX

Some four years later

It was early afternoon when he rode into Bald Hills on a lean paint gelding, the sun high overhead, the wide road through the town seen through a thin haze of dust kicked up by horsemen and trundling wagons. He rode easily, not hurrying, his eyes on the buildings on each side of that main street, on the narrower streets and alleys on both sides that led to green, open countryside that stretched for mile upon mile under clear blue skies.

He was aware of curious glances cast in his direction, and knew that certain of those observing his arrival would be astute enough to recognize his type. His clothing was dark. He wore a six-gun in a holster tied by a rawhide thong to his lean thigh. His eyes, a pale blue, moved little but saw all. And so those astute watchers would feel the stirrings of unease, and might be sufficiently troubled to drop into the jail for a quick word with the town marshal. Well, that was to be expected. If he carried the mark of an owlhoot, it had been branded

44

on him in the months he followed that trail before he had been betrayed. It was a stigma he had learned to live with, the mark of Cain, but he knew that in certain circumstances that instant recognition of the kind of man he was – a man with a perceptible aura of menace – gave him a clear advantage.

Would that advantage be needed here, in Bald Hills? Would the clear suggestion in his dress and demeanour that this was a gunslinger of considerable ability and renown – even if it was wrong – stand him in good stead?

The answer to that was that it was too early to say.

He rode past the jail without glancing in that direction, though that did not mean that every single detail of the stone building and the activity – or lack of it – was not seen, and committed to memory. The tall, skinny man, for instance. Greying of hair, a badge on his vest, his eyes also missing nothing even though he was deep in conversation with a heavily-built man of about the same age.

With the jail behind him he rode on up that wide thoroughfare, threading his way through riders, skirting wagons drawn by labouring mule teams, listening idly to the conversation of townsfolk going about their daily business – once tipping his flat-crowned grey hat to a lady who glanced in his direction only to turn away swiftly, her cheeks flushed. Then, when nothing of importance stood between him and the northern edge of the town but Barney Malone's saloon and the bank with its barred windows and heavy oak door, he turned his horse in to a hitching rail and swung out of the saddle.

End of the road. Or perhaps the beginning.

He smiled secretively, tied his horse to the rail and, spurs jingling, leaped lithely on to the plank walk. A bell tinkled as he entered the shop. As he approached the counter the lean man in the back room looked up from his workbench, wiped his oily hands on a rag and came limping through with a questioning look on his face.

'Yes sir? What can I do for you this fine day?'

The trail-worn man with the pale blue eyes frowned a little as he noticed the awkward way the gunsmith was standing. Then a slow smile softened his face.

'I need a rifle, Mr Vernon.'

'I thought you were dead. Everybody did. All this time.'

'I came close, and I've come closer many times over the years. But back then things were a mite blurred, so I'd be interested in hearing your version of events.'

The closed sign had been placed on the street door. Vernon had invited him up to the rooms he lived in above the shop. They were sitting in worn, comfortable chairs, drinking what tasted like expensive whiskey. The sun was sinking low, slanting across the table and chairs by the window, glinting on the white pitcher and bowl on the plain wooden washstand. It emphasized the bony planes of the lean gunsmith's face, caught the highlights in dark hair liberally threaded with grey.

Vernon nodded now, and when he began talking it was obvious to Red Cavanagh that he was telling a tale about which he had always been deeply troubled.

'Here in Bald Hills, we couldn't do much more than sit and listen,' Vernon said. 'From what we were told, it seems the Willis Walton boys caught up with you in that clearing down the trail, and they strung you up. Joe Parody and Flatfoot Jones were down that way, and they caught those boys in the act. Rode into the clearing. Saw you up on your horse with a rope around your neck. They were forced to back off when those outlaws opened fire. Your horse took off at the sound of gunfire, leaving you swinging. But Joe and Flatfoot, they were up against three outlaws. Outnumbered, facing crack shots, men without scruples. Parody had already taken a slug in the upper arm. There was nothing they could do to help you.'

'Is that what they told you?'

'Sure. They rode back into town. When they told their story I guess I was too shocked at the news of your death to do any straight thinking. But Parody was blustering, wanted to raise a posse. That cut no ice with me, or Lewis Edgar – who's still active on the council.' Vernon shrugged. 'Flatfoot, he stayed here in town. I rode back down the trail with Parody. So did Morris Clark, the banker, for which I would later be mighty thankful. The point is when we got to the clearing there was no sign of a hanging. A scarred branch, sure, but no rope, no body. Joe Parody had sharp eyes. He spotted something; we went into the woods, found a grave. That seemed to settle it. If we were to believe our eyes, they'd cut you down, buried you, then split a log, made a cross and stuck it in the soil. "*Red Cavanagh. Aged 17 years*".'

'Get Parody up here.'

'Parody's dead. The Willis Walton boys, when we got down there that day they hadn't cleared out. Or one of them stayed behind for some damn reason. There was a gunfight – hell, that's making it sound more than it was, just a few shots fired in an exchange that proved deadly. The outlaw was plugged by Morris Clark, but not before he shot Parody plumb between the eyes and put a slug in my leg that shattered the bone.'

'Flatfoot?'

'He's town marshal now. Has been since that terrible day.'

'Should have been you.'

'It was, for a few hours. But that outlaw's slug as good as crippled me, and a lawman needs two good legs.'

Red took a sip of whiskey, swallowed, shook his head.

'Turn that story Parody told you on its head,' he said, 'and you come to the truth.'

'Yeah, well, you've been dead four years but now you're sitting in my chair, drinking my whiskey, so clearly something stinks to high heaven.'

'Of course it does. Joe Parody and Flatfoot got there first and tried to arrest me for my pa's murder. I resisted. The reason Parody was nursing a bloody gash in his arm is because a slug from my six-gun came that close to killing him. But I was a green kid. They split up, and I was caught cold when Flatfoot came at me from behind. Yes, I was up on my sorrel like you said, but it was Flatfoot who put the rope around my neck, Flatfoot holding the horse still.'

'And then?'

'I'm up on my horse. The rope's tight. I'm going blue in the face, fighting for breath and scared rigid that Parody's going to give the signal for Flatfoot to let go and step back out of the way. Then I hear horses. Twist to have a look, and damn me if those three Willis Walton men didn't come riding down the trail and into the clearing. Flatfoot panicked. Damn near dropped his gun. He grabbed for it, forgot it was cocked, and when it went off it sounded like a charge of dynamite.'

'That's something I don't understand,' Vernon said. 'Flatfoot Jones, panicking? It hurts me to say this, but for the past four years that man has been the best, the calmest, the most level-headed marshal Bald Hills has ever had.'

'Believe me, that man went whiter than a ghost's ghost. Fired his pistol without realizing he'd done it, and the next thing I recall is the sorrel's gone from under me, there's a red haze and a roaring in my ears and horses jostling and three men up real close, two holding me to take the weight off my neck, the other one cutting the rope.

'They saved your life?'

'Damn right.'

'You told me those men killed your pa. You'd sworn to kill them. Did this act of mercy change anything?'

Red Cavanagh smiled. 'You could say that.'

'Yes, of course. You were alive.' Vernon shook his head. 'But that's not what I meant.'

He paused, swirled the whiskey in his glass, his lips pursed thoughtfully as he watched the amber liquid.

'Some ten years ago, when the Willis Walton gang were robbing banks, trains, stage coaches, there were always four of them. Then they went quiet. Four years ago, three of them rode up here to see your pa. The

49

next day they robbed the bank here in Bald Hills.'

Red nodded. 'I know.'

Vernon paused, waited for elaboration. None came.

'A few days after the fracas in the clearing that left me with a shattered leg,' he said, 'news filtered through of another bank robbery, this one in Nebraska, Boulder City. It was carried out by the Willis Walton gang. The newspaper report mentioned three men. But after saving your life, Dustin Walton died, shot by Morris Clark. That left two: Cole Willis and another I can't name.'

'Vin Devlin.'

'Yes, that's right.' Vernon paused. 'Flatfoot reckoned the fourth man joined Willis and Devlin in Boulder City, bringing the numbers back up to three.'

'Sounds reasonable.'

'Sounds impossible. Flatfoot thinks otherwise, but wasn't your pa the original fourth man? Surely that's why they rode up here to see him? You know it—'

'Do I?'

'Isn't that what happened? They'd planned the robbery of Morris Clark's bank in Bald Hills. The way I read it, they rode in to see your pa out of courtesy, offered him the chance of joining them so it'd be just like old times, then got riled when he turned them down flat.'

'No,' Red said, 'that's not what happened.'

'Then if I've got it wrong, if your pa wasn't the fourth member of the gang – and never was – then why did they ride out to the cabin? Why was there an argument?'

Vernon waited. When nothing more was forthcoming,

he shrugged his shoulders.

'Well, I'm still firmly of the opinion that in the years when they were an active gang your pa was the fourth man – but we know that when they robbed the bank in Boulder City he'd been a full two weeks dead.' Vernon flicked a fingernail against his empty glass. It rang musically. He placed it on the floor. 'So, on the day the Boulder City bank was robbed, where were you, Red?'

'It's a long time ago. I'd have to do some thinking.'

'The way they worked those bank robberies,' Vernon said, 'one man was always left holding the horses. That's the way it was done here in Bald Hills.'

Red nodded.

'One of those three bank robbers died in Boulder City,' Vernon said softly, 'because when he tried to mount his horse the saddle slipped, leaving him flat on his back. But if one man with his eyes peeled for trouble was holding the horses, how did someone get close enough to slice through that saddle's cinch with a sharp knife?'

'Maybe it wasn't like that. Cinches work loose. They wear out, sweat rots them and they snap.'

'Not according to Boulder City's marshal. It was a clean cut.'

'If you say so.'

'I do. And I also say it's ridiculous to suggest a reckless Boulder City resident sneaked up that close waving a knife. Which leaves us with the only logical alternative: the man left holding the horses stepped down and cut the cinch,' Vernon said, his penetrating gaze fixed on Cavanagh.

Red smiled. 'Go on.'

'Two outlaws came running out of that bank, made for the horses being held by the third man. One died when his saddle slipped. Two got clean away.'

'Never to be heard of again.'

Vernon shrugged. 'Four years is a long time. Men grow old and die, men die before they have a chance to grow old. But what we know for sure is that of those outlaws who rode away from Boulder City, one was Cole Willis and the other was the man who'd been holding the horses.'

'The man who, you say, is the man who cut his partner's cinch.'

'Did he?' Vernon shrugged his shoulders. 'You tell me.' He paused. 'Those two men who got away, where are they now?'

'You're building a story from facts and conjecture. If there's bits missing, I can't help you.'

'Devlin was identified as the man who died in Boulder. Cole Willis was one of the men who got away. But who was the man who rode with him, Red?'

'You're also asking questions I can't possibly answer,' Red said, 'unless I was there. Is that what you're suggesting?'

Vernon sighed wearily. 'A young man I believed dead has come back to life. You don't know how much that pleases me. As for the rest, the unanswered questions. . . .'

'That's the way they'll stay. For now, anyway.'

'I know this Cole Willis is one of the men you set out to kill. I find it hard to believe that in a little over four years you didn't get close to him.'

Red smiled. 'A man has limited powers, and they can be further restricted by circumstances. He can only do what's possible at any given time,' he said enigmatically.

'There's some sense in that,' Vernon admitted. 'Remember Grant Logan?'

'Of course.'

It was Vernon's turn to smile. 'Beth's pa, so yes, you would remember him – and that young woman's still around, by the way, still unattached. But Logan, he lost a lot of money when the Willis Walton boys robbed Morris Clark's bank and killed his boy. Took a while for his business to recover.'

'The memories I have are of a strong, ambitious man it would be hard to keep down.'

Vernon chewed on that, nodded agreement, then looked keenly at Cavanagh.

'I guess it's time to ask the one question that's been intriguing me since you walked into the shop: what brought you back to Bald Hills, Red?'

'Maybe I'm just plain weary of drifting. Maybe I heard there was trouble in Bald Hills, got a notion in my head that if I came home I could do something to help.'

'A noble cause.'

'That sounds like sarcasm.'

Vernon shook his head. 'Unintended. My day has been rocked, I'm finding it hard to take everything in. But you're right, there is trouble.'

'Caused by a powerful man who'll take some stopping.'

'If you know that much,' Vernon said, 'you must know

his name.'

Red shook his head, and stood up.

'No, I don't. But by this time tomorrow I will, and he'll know mine.'

Vernon went down the stairs after Red Cavanagh. He reached the door as the young man he'd thought dead swung into the saddle and turned his horse away from the hitch rail and up the street towards the edge of town and the trail leading to the cabin that he probably still thought of as home. The gunsmith watched until he was out of sight, then sighed.

In the late afternoon sunshine he began rolling a cigarette. The fine tobacco was caught and lifted by the warm breeze. Vernon screwed up the paper angrily, flicked it away from him and hooked his thumbs in his belt.

Dammit! He'd asked a lot of questions of the young man, but had told him nothing. That was a mistake. Because of it, when Red rode out of the woods and entered the cabin he hadn't seen since he walked out, leaving his pa lying dead on the floor, he was going to get one hell of a shock. But, more than that, he would be walking into a situation fraught with danger.

As he shook his head and turned back into his shop, Vernon couldn't help remembering a day four years ago when he had refused to sell the young Red Cavanagh a rifle. Because of his mistake, the kid had come close to death. Would this second mistake be the end of him?

SEVEN

When Red Cavanagh turned off the trail from Bald Hills and took the short uphill track to the cabin where his father had died, he saw nothing unexpected. Four years is a long time. He was quite certain that, on that tragic day, the lean gunsmith John Vernon had ridden up from the town to verify Red's story of a brutal killing. Since then there had been no reason for anyone to make that short ride. So the track was overgrown, ruts filled in, ridges flattened by weather. In some places the grass was tall and thick, brushing his stirrups, causing his horse to lift its head and snort its displeasure. Flies were everywhere, buzzing, harassing, and the trailing branches of trees brushed his shoulders. One dislodged his hat so that it fell back, held by the plaited cord, another snapped back into his face sharply enough to bring tears to his eyes.

The thought that he had to fight to get to his own home had him grinning crookedly when he came out of the trees into the yard fronting the cabin, but there the grin faded to be replaced by a puzzled frown. He drew rein without haste, folded his hands on the horn as his horse came to a standstill, took stock of the situation.

If the trail was overgrown, then the yard should have shown similar signs of neglect. But it was tidy – tidier, Red admitted, than it had ever been when Louis Cavanagh had been scratching a living wherever he could and looking after his growing son. Weeds had been ruthlessly ripped from the hard-packed earth. Shrubs close to the house had been pruned, the gallery had been swept and somebody had repaired a rail that had been broken for as long as Red could remember.

That last observation led Red's eyes to the front door. It was standing open and he could see that with fading sunlight lengthening the shadows, somebody had lit an oil lamp. And even as that shock registered, he heard the soft welcoming whicker of a horse. He glanced across at the small corral and saw a well-groomed chestnut pony standing with its head over the top rail.

When he looked back at the cabin, a tall young woman with rich dark hair had stepped out on to the gallery and was staring hard at him with huge brown eyes. The knuckles of one hand were pressed to her mouth.

Red took a deep breath and swung down from the saddle. As he led his horse to the rail he could feel his heart thumping. He took a moment to steady his nerves, fiddling clumsily to tie the reins with his gloved hands, then turned and climbed the three steps. He could hear the thud of his boots, the jingle of his spurs, the faint slap of his holster against his thigh, the whisper of his pulse in his ears. Every sound was magnified in a silence that suggested the world had suddenly come to a stop, and was holding its breath.

'Red?' the young woman said hesitantly, her dark eyes brimming.

He nodded, unable to speak.

Then he took a quick step forwards and she seemed to tumble into his arms. Her fingers were around his back and clutching at his shirt and her face was against his chest as she sobbed brokenly.

'John Vernon was uncertain, but I was always convinced you were still alive.'

'I—'

'Why didn't you get in touch? Let me know?'

He shrugged helplessly.

'You didn't want to? Couldn't? Though how anything could stop you at least sending a letter I do not know. You had four years, Red. When you left you were not long out of school. Did you all at once forget how to write?'

'I . . . couldn't find the words. If I'd put pen to paper it would have helped neither of us.'

He knew it was a lame answer, but when he looked into her eyes he realized she was teasing him, saw nothing there but love. She would want to know everything, of course she would, but in the fifteen minutes or so since Red had ridden up to the cabin and she had fallen into his arms it had become clear that nothing had changed. Though no longer children, they were still young. Wiser, certainly, because in that part of the world growing up fast was a necessity if a person was to

57

stay alive and in good health. But that wisdom had told them ever more clearly during the long years of separation that the troth they had made as children was a troth made for life.

But. . . . Whatever that would lead to could wait, would have to wait. Red shook his head, saw her gentle, quizzical look and grinned.

'Mixed up, I said, and that was the truth. But if I was mixed up before I got here, right now I'm totally confused. Beth, what on earth are you doing living in my house?'

'Perhaps it's now my house. A dead man cannot own property. By moving in, taking up permanent residency, it's possible I can claim right of ownership.'

They were sitting in the familiar living room. The oil lamp Beth had lit stood on the dark wood chiffonier. It cast a warm glow over worn but comfortable chairs, the rough stone of the fireplace that had been Louis Cavanagh's pride, the soft animal skins covering the floor.

Red looked around him, then back at Beth with his eyebrows raised in consternation.

'Is that true?'

'I've no idea.' She grinned briefly, letting him know she was still teasing, then quickly became serious. 'Besides, the real truth is that I moved in because I could no longer bear to be close to my father.'

'What on earth has he done? Grant Logan always was a hard man,' Red acknowledged, 'but—'

'Hard was something I could live with. You'll remember my mother died when I was very young, so in a way

58

that rock-like quality my father had always made me feel secure. The hardness is still there, but in the past year he's become a grim man with cold eyes and a ruthless streak in him that is truly horrific. That's something I cannot stand.'

'Ruthlessness in men like your father usually shows itself in the way they do business. Is that what you mean, Beth? I know there are homesteads and small ranches all around Bald Hills. What's he doing, fencing off the water, driving their livestock off rich pasture?'

'Perhaps that's a method he'll use. In his present mood I expect almost anything. He's set out to acquire all the land as far as the eye can see, especially to the north of the town,' she said.

Red frowned. 'I seem to remember he was always keen on expanding to the north, wasn't he? Always had that dream of making the Slash L the biggest brand in southern Wyoming.'

'If that was his aim it would be understandable, yes, even if I disproved of the methods. But that's only part of it. As well as land, he's going after the town itself. He's taking over businesses, one by one. If the owners won't sell, he drives them out by one means or another.'

'Then I don't understand. It's as if . . . I don't know, as if an already ambitious man has suddenly gone power crazy.'

'It *was* sudden,' Beth said, 'and that's why I'm puzzled. One day he was my father, Grant Logan, tough but fair; the next he was this stranger with naked greed in his eyes.'

Red cocked his head. 'Greed?'

'Yes.' Beth nodded. 'Business of any kind is always about money, isn't it? But what I don't understand is where the big ideas came from, where they're taking him, where all this money is going to come from.'

'What about your brother Rick? He's older than you by, what, three or four years, isn't he? What does he think of the change? Whose side is he on?'

'Mine, in a sense. By that I mean he's also uneasy about what Dad's doing and would perhaps leave the spread if he could, but that would be deserting Dad. Rick's Slash L foreman now. The trouble is we both know he's getting dragged into something he has no stomach for. There'll come a time, quite soon, when he too says enough is enough.'

'But until then. . . .'

For a few minutes they were both lost in thought. Beth rose from her chair and went into the kitchen. Red heard the clink of crockery, and knew she was pouring coffee from the pot she had earlier set on the big iron stove. He crossed to the window, looked across the yard to the trees and realized he had left his horse tied at the rail and still saddled.

Well, he would take care of that shortly, strip the rig and dump it in the small barn, let the horse loose in the corral with the friendly chestnut. Yet the thought of doing that led to the realization that he and Beth were faced with a problem that needed sorting out before nightfall. He pursed his lips, tapped them thoughtfully with his finger, then turned from the window as Beth returned.

'Who knows you're living here?'

'Nobody.'

She handed him a steaming mug and he gasped as it burnt his fingers.

'From what you just said I thought you and Rick had talked things over. Didn't you tell him your plans?'

'Yes, I did, but I trust him to keep it to himself. And nobody else can possibly know because of the way I went about it. All Dad knew was that I was riding into town. Once there I called in the general store and bought enough supplies for a couple of weeks.'

'That would have appeared strange.'

'I told Molly we'd run short of a few things.'

Red grinned. 'And you, a prosperous rancher's daughter, were carrying potatoes and cabbages back home in a sack.'

'If that's what she thought, she was too busy to comment. When I left the store I rode on up the street, and. . . .'

She paused, bit her lip. Red waited.

'Go on, you rode up the street, and. . . ?'

'I've been pretty close to John Vernon ever since the time he rode out to see me and gave me your message.'

' "*My leaving has been forced on me by tragedy, I'll be gone a few days at most*".' Red grimaced.

'Your memory's as good as mine. The nice thing is if we both recall it so clearly that tells us everything about how we've always felt for each other. Anyway, it didn't work out the way we both wanted it to, but please don't ever regret saying it. Those words were what I clung to for four years.'

'I certainly gave "a few days" a whole new meaning,'

Red said gruffly.

'Yes, well, John Vernon did all he could to recover your body when everybody thought you'd been hanged. I've been close to him since that terrible day and—'

'And he knows you're here, in this house.'

She nodded. 'Yes, he does. Apart from anything else, I thought it wise to let at least one other person know in case something went wrong. You know, a woman out here, on her own.' She saw him nod acceptance, and went on, 'But now it's my turn. Who knows *you're* here, Red?'

'Same question, same answer. The last person to see me when I left Bald Hills was John Vernon. I thought it only right that he should be the first to see me on my return.'

She was watching him closely. 'Why did you stay away so long, Red? What happened to bring you back? And why now?'

He sighed. 'The simple answer is that the impossible became possible. Suddenly there was nothing stopping me, and when that moment arrived. . . .' He spread his hands. 'Well, here I am.'

'And does it feel right?'

'Nothing I have ever done,' Red said, 'has pleased me more, or brought me more . . . joy, happiness . . . I'm lost for words, can't believe it's happening. It just feels so good it's as if I'm dreaming, and I'm scared that any moment now I'll wake up and be back to cruel reality.'

'I know, I feel like pinching myself too.' Beth smiled happily. 'Anyway, we can be together here in this house for tonight at least, Red – in separate bedrooms, of course,' she added, blushing. 'It's late summer; tomorrow's sure to be another warm day. We can take our time talking over what we're going to do, and then, when that's done – well, there's more, isn't there. You've told me the simple reason why you came back. Tomorrow, when the time is right, you can tell me exactly what happened to make it possible for you to return to Bald Hills.'

EIGHT

He thought at first that it was Beth moving about, perhaps making a hot drink, and for a few brief moments in the cold clear light of early dawn he lay on his back in bed listening contentedly. Then, as he came fully awake, he knew the sounds were all wrong. Beth would have padded from her room to the kitchen on bare feet, or perhaps wearing soft moccasins. What Red could hear as he started up in bed was the sound of hard-booted feet moving quickly, muffled briefly as they crossed the living-room's thick animal-skin rugs, then louder and much closer as they approached his bedroom door.

The sharp rap on the woodwork sent him rolling out of bed and up on to his feet. He was in his long underwear, naked from the waist up, barefoot. Still sluggish, half awake, he hesitated before recalling where he'd left his gunbelt and starting around the bed to where it hung on the chair by the open window.

He was too late.

The iron latch clicked, the door crashed open to a

violent kick. A man almost as wide as the door's opening lifted a six-gun and thumbed back the hammer with an oily snap. Red, still going for his gun, looked back over his shoulder and saw other men crowding the living room behind the intruder.

'Your hand touches that gun,' the big man said, 'you'll save yourself a whipping by dying of lead poisoning.'

'A whipping?'

Red stopped, still an arm's length away from his gunbelt.

'If a man is sleeping with your daughter, what would you do to him?'

'You're either blind or stupid. Can you see anyone else in that bed? Besides, you're not—'

'Outside.'

The man waggled the six-gun, took a step back.

Red sucked in a deep breath, straightened to his full height. He was, he realized, taller than the man with a gun. Probably a lot fitter. Certainly faster. His gun was within reach. Beyond the open window it was maybe fifty feet to the trees. . . .

As if reading his mind, the big man grinned.

'Do as you're told, now, or I'll plug you anyway. I don't suppose Mr Logan'd care too much either way.'

Red swore softly. He padded around the bed and brushed past the big man as he stood to one side. When he stepped out of the room he received a violent push in the back. He staggered forwards, slipped on one of the rugs and almost fell. Two men grabbed him by the arms. He was half run, half carried across the room.

They threw him bodily out of the cabin on to the gallery. He went down, hitting the boards hard and instinctively rolling. He felt the skin tearing on his naked shoulder. Disorientated, he was shaking his head to clear it when he was once more grabbed, hauled forward and thrown down the short flight of steps. This time he landed heavily on hard-packed dirt. He grunted as most of the breath was driven from his body. His head cracked against a stone. Behind his eyes, red light flared.

'Take him,' another, deeper voice said, 'and tie him to the corral's top pole so I can see his back.'

The words were accompanied by an eerie whisper of sound, punctuated by a sharp crack like a gunshot.

Red felt his mouth go dry.

They picked him up again and dragged him across the yard. His toes scraped across the dirt. He thought of struggling, but what was the use? Two men had hard hands clamped on his arms. Another man as big as a house was holding a cocked six-gun. There were more, three or four of them; he could hear horses, the jingle of bridles, men muttering.

And then there was Grant Logan.

Red was slammed against the corral's poles. The men holding him yanked his arms to the side so that they were painfully outstretched. Then the other men he had heard came in close and roughly tied his wrists to the pole with what felt like wet rawhide.

'All right, now step back out of the way.'

The eerie whisper, swish. The sharp crack.

'You know what that is, Cavanagh?' Grant Logan said. Without thinking, Red found some saliva in his

66

mouth, turned his head sideways and spat into the dirt.

Somebody laughed, the sound instantly altered to sound like a cough.

Red lifted his head. It was a small corral. One of the riders had walked his horse around the side so that he could look across and see Red's face. It was Rick Logan, Beth's brother. Older by those four years Red had been absent, but not much changed. A dark, handsome face, now looking troubled. Possibly guilty. Somebody had told his father where Beth was hiding. Could it have been Rick?

'It's a whip,' Grant Logan said, cutting through his thoughts, 'and I'm about to use it to make you pay for what you've done. Do you know what that is?'

'Your man said something about me sleeping with your daughter. He was wrong.'

'Oh, no, he was right. This is your house. You were in there all night, and so was my daughter.'

'We were in separate rooms, nothing happened.'

'In the eyes of the world,' Grant Logan said, 'the mere fact that you two spent the night together tells a story not open to misinterpretation.'

Red laughed shortly. 'You're a big man, Logan. I've never known you to care a damn for other people's opinions.'

'So this is a moment for you to savour.'

'Ask her. Ask your daughter. If you don't believe me, surely you'll believe your own flesh and blood?'

'She's not here.'

'But—'

'She was taken away before you were woken.'

'How? I'm a light sleeper. Out of necessity. For one reason or another, the past four years have taught me that was the only way to stay alive, or at least to stay one piece. So how can that be?'

'That's no longer your concern. By now my daughter's safely back home where she belongs. That's as it should be. No sensitive female should be forced to stand by and watch a grown man being horsewhipped.'

'Or anyone else not on your payroll, is that—'

Red's words were chopped off as the next whisper of sound was immediately followed by a searing streak of fire across the centre of his back. No crack, this time, but something that sounded like a man's face being slapped by an irate saloon girl. It was thin, plaited rawhide being laid with the full power of Grant Logan's strong right arm across his naked skin, but an involuntary grin pulled at his lips even as his head jerked backwards in agony. A grunt was forced through his clenched teeth. Through eyes squeezed tight with pain he squinted blindly into the corral as his horse kicked up its hoofs in fright and galloped to the far rails to stand there quivering, ears flattened, nostrils flaring.

Again the whisper of sound through the air, the slap, again the streak of fire. Red's wrists jerked against the rawhide binding him to the pole. His fists were clenched, nails digging into his palms. Deliberately, he increased the pressure on his arms, tensing his muscles, pulling against the rawhide. The lash descended again, then again, the leather of the lash like a razor. Red felt the skin rip, the first trickle of hot blood, bit his lip until it bled as Logan warmed to the task and put more weight into the cruel beating.

But now Red had three sources of pain. The rawhide binding him was biting into both wrists. The pain there was his to control. Red concentrated on it, deliberately sagged so that his own weight was added to the pull his muscles were exerting. In that way he was able to put the relentless cutting of the whip to the back of his mind, to drift on the searing pain of his wrists with a twisted grin of contempt baring his red-stained teeth and his eyes staring without seeing at the expanse of dirt and the shifting shadow of his frightened horse.

He reacted almost with surprise when, after time that had no meaning, Logan finally wearied of effort that was bringing him no visible reward. But by then Red's crude mind games had gone beyond telling him that the pain was receding into the background, because conscious-ness had for some time been mercifully slipping away. His head was down, hanging, his chin digging into his chest. And he heard voices, as if in a dream. . . .

'Where the hell are you going?'

'Into town. I've had enough, you sicken me.'

A harsh laugh. 'Come to terms with it, Rick—'

'This was inhuman. You know Beth's done nothing wrong, and if she hasn't then neither has he.'

'I know you told me where I could find her on the same day this sonofabitch came crawling back home.'

To that there was no answer other than a muted curse.

Then the sound of hoofs, fast fading into silence.

Another voice, gruff, questioning. Then Grant Logan's again.

'No, leave him be. The sun will be up shortly. He'll appreciate the warmth on his back.'

A harsh laugh. The creak of a saddle. More hoof-beats.

Then nothing. . . .

NINE

Grant Logan lingered for a while close to Red Cavanagh's cabin so that the other members of the group could ride ahead of him through the thin woods to the west of the house. The trail on the other side of the timber wound through undulating terrain well away from Lost Creek. The men were already out of sight when he emerged from the trees, and he knew they'd be scattered about the ranch when he reached the Slash L.

Riding in alone was a habit that had grown into an obsession. No matter how little time he had been away, he liked to approach his sprawling spread without company and in his own good time so that he could savour in solitude the empire he had built through sheer guts, determination and an iron will that would tolerate nothing less than success.

Today he felt it especially important to adhere to that routine, for he was nervously aware that momentous changes were drawing very close. Not here. He had

71

made damn sure that those changes, which he was mas-terminding and which would bring him wealth beyond even his wildest dreams, would affect only the outermost acres of Slash L's sprawling pastures.

The Slash L premises stood for permanence, and as he approached, he gazed with pride at the single-storey, white-painted timber ranch house set back against a stand of trees, the huge yard almost encircled by massive barns and a long low bunkhouse. Beyond those buildings several corrals were all that stood between the house and the lush grassland to the west and north.

Every square mile, as far as the horizon and beyond, belonged to the Slash L and thus to Grant Logan. Very soon, some of that land would be sold. The sale was part of a grand scheme that, taken as a whole, would make him rich.

As he rode unhurriedly towards the house, a tall man came down the steps. He stood waiting by the hitch rail, one hand resting on the sleek neck of a big blue roan that stood dozing in the warm sunshine. His presence seemed to snap Grant Logan back to tense reality. He swung down, tied his horse alongside the tall man's roan, then briefly lifted his gaze to the land to the north. His eyes hardened. The smile that curled his thin lips was cruel, the look in his eyes so ruthless that any man seeing it would have felt his blood run cold.

'She settled?'

'She's not caused any trouble. I've got a couple of good men watching. She tries to make a run for it she'll find her way blocked gently but firmly.'

'They're my men,' Logan said. 'I know them all. You don't have to tell me if they're good or bad.'

'I meant no offence. But I am here at your request, to do a job that I understand is beyond the capabilities of any man on your payroll.'

'You're a gunman, Warrener. If necessary, you shoot to kill. That requires a frame of mind men don't get from punching cattle.'

Chet Warrener grinned. 'Killing is just one of my many and varied talents, as you've just found out.'

'Which means you can take liberties with me?'

'For God's sake,' the tall man said, 'you asked a question and you got my answer. The fact that your daughter's here at all is down to my good work.'

'But my planning.'

'True. But where exactly does that planning lead? What comes next?'

Logan jerked his head and pointed to a glade in the trees behind the house where fallen logs had been trimmed, then rolled across the grass to serve as seats. When he had the time, he would stroll up on to that rise and enjoy the late evening sunshine with a glass of fine whiskey glinting in his hand.

'We'll talk up there,' he said, and turned away to set off up the gentle slope.

The tall man followed without haste.

He was broad-shouldered, heavily muscled, grey-haired. Despite the powerful build, the way he moved hinted at the ability to leap into action with startling speed. He had lightning-fast hands, and that talent had served him well in the past, had sent several men to early graves, but had bred in him remarkable arrogance. Chet Warrener had his initials burned into the leather of the holster holding his Colt .44, carved into the bone handle of that weapon, and stitched on the worn leather vest that hung without shape from his broad shoulders.

Watching Warrener's slow stroll up the slope to join him, Logan was restless. He kicked irritably at one of the heavy logs, stalked with his thumb hooked in his gunbelt to gaze once again to the north. The comfort gained from his solitary approach to the Slash L had been wiped out when sight of Chet Warrener and the words they had exchanged had driven home the stark reality of what he had done.

He had arranged for his own daughter to be snatched against her will, using the excuse of rescuing her from an immediate future spent living in sin with Red Cavanagh to test the man Warrener's bold claim. The gunman had been quite clear, even dismissive. He had the ability, he had said, to move at night as silently and as stealthily as a cat, whether in open country, through a sleeping town, or through the interior of a strange building where all lights had been extinguished. Nothing to it. Hell, he'd been doing it since he was a kid stealing cookies on his family's farm in northern Texas.

As soon as Warrener had made the claim, Grant Logan felt an idea take shape in his mind and emerge fully formed. The answer to the one problem dogging him – the removal of the last and seemingly immovable obstacle blocking the path to immense riches – had been handed to him on a plate. It involved cruelty. If the rewards had not been so great, Logan admitted, even a man as ruthless as he might have baulked at the actions required.

It was a plan that could not fail. However, there were still some details to be worked out. In the meantime. . . .

He swung to face the gunman, who had dropped on to one of the logs and was watching him with mild amusement in his grey eyes.

'What comes next,' Logan said, 'is the removal of a minor irritation a couple of miles to the north of Slash L. Two brothers, Dan'l and Gray Ford, own a small spread. One boundary is Lost Creek, another is the A Bar F, Alan Forsyth's spread. The brothers are in financial trouble. They've sold most of their stock. I've made them a generous offer, which they've turned down flat.'

'Irritating.'

'Foolhardy. You're going there this evening. You'll take with you my less generous offer, in cash.'

'And if they still refuse?'

'A certain kind of armed man riding in out of the dark should be menacing enough. If not...' Logan shrugged his shoulders. 'They'll have a shotgun, somewhere. Men like that, they're more likely to remember where they've put their hoe, so if you have some digging to do. . . .'

'Me, I've always favoured the nearest river when disposing of rubbish,' Warrener said. He looked hard at Logan. 'If all I'm doing is riding out to make a couple of homesteaders see the error of their ways,' he said, 'what the hell was all that about this morning?'

'That was about testing a rock solid way of making a

stubborn, powerful rancher come to exactly the same conclusion,' Logan said, and he took another kick at the log and started back down the slope.

TEN

A hard hand came out of nowhere to grasp his wrist. He tensed, felt the touch of cold steel. The rawhide binding his right arm to the pole parted. His arm dropped to his side and he groaned as the altered position sent pain ripping through cramped muscles.

'Easy, boy,' a familiar, caring voice said.

John Vernon, the gunsmith.

Vernon was standing very close behind him. Red felt warm breath on the skin at the back of his neck. A hip was thrust hard up against the bottom of his spine, holding him against the corral's peeled poles without the need to touch his naked back. The lean man behind him reached over, a hand grasped his other wrist and the sharp blade did its work.

Red felt his knees begin to buckle.

'Take your time,' John Vernon said. 'Grip the rail, I'll help support you. When you feel able to walk, let me know.'

Red's eyes were closed. He knew that on the other side of the rail his Paint horse was standing close to him.

The animal had trotted across the corral soon after Grant Logan had departed. As the first hour passed, then the second, its bulk had been a shield standing between Red and the increasing heat of the sun.

Without that, he thought absently, I would have died. A smile twitched his dry lips. Perhaps he had. Did dead men dream? He opened his eyes, blinked a couple of times to clear them and looked at the dust of the corral, made the effort and raised his head so he could see the far rails and the rich green of the trees.

'OK,' Red said after a while. His voice was hoarse. He cleared his throat. 'OK,' he said again, 'let's try it.'

And he turned away from the rail, unsteadily, to hang on to John Vernon's wiry arm all the way across the small yard and into the cool shadows of the cabin.

'He didn't rip the skin,' Vernon said.

'Could've sworn I felt blood.'

'Heat creating an illusion. All right, so the bastard did cut you in a couple of places. But the rest is raw weals. Mostly you're suffering from shock, exposure; any longer out there in that sun and you'd have been in trouble.'

'So what kept you?'

Vernon chuckled. He was using warm water and a soft cloth to clean Red's back, working as tenderly as a woman.

'Rick couldn't find me. He was feeling guilty enough to want to get help to you, but not bad enough to let people know what his pa had done. He tracked me to the café where I'd enjoyed a late breakfast, was told

78

there I'd gone down to talk to Flatfoot Jones at the jail. That made it difficult to get his message across without telling the whole world. He hung around kicking his heels until I came out.'

Red was sitting at the pine table, bent forward over the cool boards with his upper body and head resting on his folded arms. He felt half asleep. The air was chill on his damp back. He sensed Vernon step away, took a deep breath and straightened gingerly. When he turned awkwardly on the chair and stood up, the gunsmith had emptied the bowl and was watching him critically.

'You'll do. Put your pants on, but leave your shirt off for the rest of today. Fresh air will take care of the healing. By tomorrow you'll have some discomfort, but you'll be moving about more easily.'

'I'm working on that now,' Red said, heading for the open front door. 'I'll be sitting in the sun on the gallery while you brew coffee.'

The roof overhung the gallery so that the chairs up against the wall of the cabin were in shade. Midday had long gone. The breeze had dropped, the air was still and warm. Red sank into a hard chair, wriggled back to find a position which left nothing above his waist touching the chair's back. He sat for ten minutes or so, feeling the tension seep out of his muscles, leaving his mind occupied with imponderables. The horsewhipping had already been dismissed as a painful irrelevance, but he wondered how Logan's men had sneaked Beth out of the house without his hearing? And other things: the information, for instance, that Vernon must have had available yesterday but hadn't thought worth passing on to him.

'When I said that by today I'd know the name of the big man causing trouble, you were a step ahead of me weren't you,' he said as Vernon came limping out on to the gallery. 'Why didn't you tell me?'

Vernon passed him a drink and sat down, nursing his cup as he stared out across the rail to the yard, the corral, the green woods.

'A long time ago you asked me for a rifle, and I refused. Ever since that day, I've felt responsible for your death. Seeing you again took away most of that guilt, but left me wary of making another mistake. What if I'd told you, and Grant Logan or one of his men had put a bullet in you?'

'One of his men? Is that leading somewhere?'

'When I was washing blood and sweat off your back I mentioned that I was talking to Flatfoot Jones when Rick caught up with me. Flatfoot told me he saw you ride in yesterday. He recognized you instantly, expressed his astonishment out loud, and it was picked up pretty quick by the man he was talking to.'

'Big feller, tall, grey hair.' Red nodded, remembering glancing that way in passing.

'His name is Chet Warrener. According to Flatfoot – these are his words – mention of your name knocked him sideways.'

'Probably means nothing more than he knows somebody whose uncle heard a friend of a friend repeating a rumour he'd overheard from a barmaid's half-breed brother in a New Mexico cantina – maybe,' Red said, grinning, but thoughtful.

His sudden disquiet was not lost on Vernon.

'Anyway,' the gunsmith said after a moment, 'Warrener appeared a couple of weeks ago, rode in out of nowhere and made straight for the Slash L. If I was asked to give him a job title, I'd say he's an enforcer. He's a gunman hired by Logan to apply pressure when it's needed.'

'As in suggesting to certain businessmen they should relinquish ownership of their premises.'

Vernon turned away from his study of the landscape to look at Red.

'Your young lady's been doing some talking.'

'Is she right?'

'Oh, yes. Denny Coburn's still running the livery barn, and his name's still on the board over the doors, but the place is owned by Logan. Same goes for the general store. Further up the street, Morris Clark's holding out, but that's hardly surprising. A bank's an entirely different proposition, and a banker's got pressures of his own he can apply; if pushed too hard, he could ruin a man.'

'And the gunsmith?'

'Not been troubled.' Vernon grinned. 'Maybe it's down to me having enough weaponry on the premises to deter even the toughest of enforcers.'

'Nevertheless, you and Clark are the exceptions. I'd guess a lot of folk will be less stubborn. Could be some will jump at the chance to sell up, if Logan's paying well.'

'If he was paying well,' John Vernon said, 'there'd be no need to hire an enforcer.'

'That's true. So, the easy way or the hard way, Grant Logan's set on taking over Bald Hills. And not just the town. According to Beth, he's also keen on acquiring land – in particular that stretching away to the north.'

Vernon frowned. 'Well, I've heard rumours to that effect. And I don't like 'em. There's a patch belonging to the Ford brothers, but the only spread of any size to the north is the A Bar F.'

'Alan Forsyth's place.'

'A man who's seen his fair share of trouble and fought his way through it all with great courage. He lost his wife, lost a heap of money when the Willis Walton gang robbed Clark's bank, his only daughter was crippled in a riding accident.'

'That would be Ellie,' Red said, remembering the flaxen-haired woman. He glanced across at Vernon, paused. 'Am I sensing something here, John?'

'Mm.' Vernon nodded. 'She walks with a stick. I've . . . we've been seeing each other for some time.'

'That must make a pretty picture.' Red grinned, nodded his head to where Vernon's stick was resting against a chair. 'You're sweet on her, John?'

'We've a lot in common,' Vernon said. 'We're both . . . damaged goods, as you've pointed out.' He smiled absently. 'What I can't understand is why she's said nothing to me about Logan's intentions.'

'Obvious answer is she doesn't know. Or maybe Logan hasn't yet made his approach. If he has, then I'd say Forsyth is shielding his daughter from bad news.'

'Forsyth won't sell.'

'Enter Chet Warrener, the enforcer.'

'Compared to what Forsyth has been through, Warrener is small potatoes.'

'Even the strongest of men,' Red said, 'has his Achilles heel.'

He saw Vernon's frown deepen, his jaw muscles bunch as his mind followed the logical progression from cash offer to threats followed by violence.

'This fellow, Warrener,' Red said. 'I don't suppose you've been in the vicinity when he's been talking to Flatfoot?'

'Difficult not to be,' Vernon said. 'I'm on the town council with Lewis Edgar, and one or the other of us drops in to see Flatfoot most days. Chet Warrener does the same, so our paths frequently cross.'

'How is it he's so cosy with Flatfoot? Didn't you say Warrener's been here no more than a couple of weeks?'

'Forget the two weeks. Putting two and two together from incidents Flatfoot's talked about or let slip, I'd say he and that gunslinger, Chet Warrener, go back at least twenty years.'

ELEVEN

The moon was bathing the Wyoming landscape in cold, eerie light. The lack of any breeze, the sheer stillness of the night, created absolute silence in which any sudden sound was magnified and distorted. A coyote's mournful howl could chill the average town dweller's blood, a crackle in the undergrowth would send his hand fumbling for his pistol as his eyes searched the shadows, the whisper of a night bird swooping low overhead might cause him to duck instinctively in the saddle then softly curse his own cowardice.

But Chet Warrener was no town dweller, and danger was his lifeblood. He had ridden the owlhoot trail, taken risks for the fun of it, laughed out loud in the face of fearsome jeopardy. Many times over the years he had narrowly escaped death, almost always in broad daylight at the hands of angry lawmen bearing down on him in some anonymous dusty street running between shabby timber false fronts. Rarely, he had been caught out in the open, trapped in deep snow or baking in the desert heat. Surrounded by a posse, his horse lathered white with exhaustion, his survival had always been down to the unusual ability to remain calm when all seemed lost, to wriggle out of situations from which there appeared to be no possibility of escape.

So it was that as he rode along the sloping grass bank close to the waters of Lost Creek, sheered away from that glittering ribbon to cross the strip of land that took him from the Slash L on to the few paltry acres owned by the Ford brothers, he was watchful, but unconcerned. The watchfulness was a habit born of a lifetime spent on the wrong side of the law. His lack of concern was down to two simple facts: the reward for his capture, dead or alive, was scrawled on wanted Dodgers pinned to noticeboards far off in the distant towns of southern Texas; in Wyoming he was a stranger, unknown, unrecognized.

But not for long, he thought ruefully. Borrowed time was not a phrase he had used often, but how else could he describe a situation that had become dangerous almost overnight? He'd been careful to say nothing to Grant Logan, but unless he now stayed well clear of Bald Hills, his past would inevitably catch up with him.

And that, Warrener admitted with a grim smile, could have a serious and permanent effect on his health.

Nevertheless, as he made his way across open grassland towards the long stretch of woodland within which he knew the Fords' house was hidden, his concentration was entirely on what lay ahead. Several times his hand drifted to his pocket to touch the bulky envelope given to him by Grant Logan, for therein lay a paradox. The envelope bore the legend Bald Hill's Bank, prop. Morris

Clark. The thick wad of banknotes it contained could be seen as a reasonable offer to buy the Fords' small spread, or as a bribe; an inducement for the brothers to leave the land, and Wyoming, with no questions asked.

As far as Chet Warrener was concerned, it was neither of those. Instead, it was money given to him as part payment for his services. When he rode away from the house, job done, the money would remain in his pocket. The inducement for the brothers to leave – though he had no intention of using it for that particular purpose – lay in the blued steel of the six-gun sitting easy in its holster, the brass shells poking their deadly noses out of the cylinder. The evidence that the man they were up against was as unstoppable as a raging winter storm lay in the arrogance of Warrener's initials carved in leather and worn bone.

But tonight he had covered those signs. To become an anonymous shape in the moonlight he had donned a duster coat. Lightweight and black, it covered him from shoulders to ankles. In it he was just another shadow.

He reached the edge of the stand of timber, cut his roan through the trees and rode into the open space of the Fords' yard. The shabby cabin was a depressing place. Tucked away as it was in dark woods, with shafts of moonlight penetrating here and there, the atmosphere surrounding it was one of gloom. In addition to the house there were just a few dilapidated sheds, an empty corral. If they owned horses, Warrener surmised, they would be standing on filthy straw in one of the draughty sheds. It mattered not a jot. The brothers were not going to use them. Warrener was – but if they knew what he proposed to do with their mounts they would already be out of the back door and fleeing like startled deer into the black woods.

Leaving the house empty. Which it would be, anyway, when his night's work was finished. And that, he thought, with a sudden flash of inspiration, would be mighty convenient if he'd correctly interpreted Grant Logan's sinister plans.

Even as the thought entered his mind and lodged there, he heard a soft whicker from one of the stabled horses and saw his roan's ears prick. Then he swung lithely down out of the saddle. He left the reins trailing in the dust. His spurs had been removed. Soundlessly he covered the last few yards to the house. He placed his hand on the door's rusty handle and walked straight in.

The stench hit him in the face. There was one smoking oil lamp. A rough table standing on packed earth, laden with greasy plates. A couple of chairs dragged close to an iron stove, glowing red, fumes leaking like poison from the cracked pipe leading to the darkness of the tin roof.

'Jesus Christ,' Warrener said softly.

Two old men had turned to look at him.

'Who the hell are you, Black Bart?'

'I'm your saviour,' he said. 'Doesn't matter what comes next, because anything's better than this.' He looked at them, at the straggly beards, the smouldering clay pipe one of them had clamped between blackened teeth, the eyes that peered at him like frightened birds. 'Which one's which?'

'I'm Dan'l,' said the man with the pipe. 'That's my brother, Gray.' He used the pipe stem to point. 'You ain't answered yet, but if you're from that devil Logan I hope you're carrying cash money.'

'Oh, I am indeed,' Warrener said. He stepped to the table, took the thick envelope from the pocket of his duster and slapped it between the greasy dishes. 'Not as much as you'd hoped for, but, hell, what can you expect when you waste his time shilly-shallying?'

'How much?'

'Count it.'

The wet stem of the pipe was poked into the torn pocket of Dan'l Ford's vest. He rose and limped to the table on worn stovepipe boots. He licked blunt, filthy fingers, riffled through the bills, looked up at Warrener in disgust.

'The man's either a skinflint or a crook.'

'And there ain't a shadow of doubt one of them bad names fits as easy as another,' Gray said, almost spitting the words.

'A receipt,' Warrener said implacably, 'scrawled in pencil if you can find one and with an X if you can't sign your name, will see an end to this.'

'Do it, Dan'l,' Gray Ford growled.

He came out of his chair in a rolling motion. A big man with huge shoulders, he went to a sagging shelf, located a notebook, a stub of pencil. He threw them on the table. Dan'l sat down, licked the pencil, found a clean page and began to write.

'Put down Logan's name, so it's clear to all who's bought this rat-infested hell hole,' Warrener said. 'Also the generous sum he's paid.'

'Thievin' sonofabitch,' Dan'l grunted.

Warrener grinned.

'This hands the spread over to him, all nice and legal,' Dan'l said, ripping out the sheet. 'Ain't no deeds, far as I know, but how could there be,' and he cackled. 'Lyin' there between A Bar F, Slash L and Lost Creek, it always was wasted land. But possession's nine points of the law, ain't that what they say? So that made it ours, and we hung on to it for nigh on fifteen years.'

'And now it's Grant Logan's,' Warrener said. He looked thoughtfully around the room, at the pitiful possessions. 'I don't see a wagon out there. What are you two taking with you?'

'Nary a thing,' Grant said. 'So feel free to look around, friend, if there's anything here you fancy. . . .'

Warrener smiled grimly. He took the paper from Dan'l, glanced at the scrawled writing, the illegible signature, pulled aside the duster to stuff it into the vest pocket bearing his initials. Then he reached over with a gloved hand and scooped up the envelope containing the cash.

'What the hell—'

Warrener took a short step backwards, the envelope in his left hand. Dan'l Ford's bloodshot eyes widened in disbelief. Gray took in the situation at a glance. He swore, turned fast towards the corner where a shotgun leaned against the wall. Warrener bared his teeth in a friendly grin. A swift right hand swept the duster out of the way. Then, as smoothly as a woman's hand emerging from a purse of pure silk, the bone-handled six-gun leaped into his hand.

Two shots cracked, the detonations in the cramped room ringing musically in the big black stove. Gray, one hand reaching for the scattergun, was knocked backwards against the glowing iron. He hit hard, his weight forcing him down against the hot metal. There was a faint sizzle, the smell of burning cloth. Then, with a solid thump, he was on his back on the dirt floor. His eyes stared vacantly. One booted foot twitched.

Dan'l was closer to Warrener. The slug hit him dead centre, drilling through his breastbone. Breath exploded from his gaping mouth. He took the chair with him as he flew backwards from the table. One trailing sleeve dragged the greasy tin plates. They bounced and clattered across the floor. The chair splintered as Dan'l went down. One plate rolled slowly, tipped over and spun noisily to stillness. In the sudden heavy silence that descended on the room just one man's ragged breathing could be heard.

Chet Warrener dragged a hand across his face. He took a deep breath, and pouched the six-gun.

'And now,' he said into the hot, foetid silence, 'comes a spell of backbreaking hard work.'

He slipped out of the duster and draped it over a chair, then went out into the night leaving the front door open. Working by moonlight, he led the two horses out of the almost derelict barn behind the house. Their worn saddles were hanging on a broken rail. He carried them outside one by one, saddled the two horses and led them around to the front of the house. Then he went back inside.

First he straightened the mess. The greasy plates went back on the table. The splintered chair he could do nothing to repair. He simply leant it drunkenly against the table, and grinned at the sight: in that room where almost everything was falling apart, the damage would go unnoticed.

He took a last swift look around. It told him that, because the two men had died instantly, not a drop of blood had been spilled. Then he dealt with Dan'l. He took hold of the dead man's ankles and dragged him roughly out of the front door, bumped him down the step and hauled him to the nearest horse. Despite the animal's uneasiness the thin body was easily hoisted up and draped limply over the saddle. Gray Ford was a different proposition. He was as heavy as a felled steer. His head bumped sickeningly down the step. When Warrener tried to heave him over the saddle he got the dead weight as high as the stirrups then was forced to let go.

He stood back, settled his breathing, then spat on his gloves and tried again. Using the full strength of his arms and a desperate shove from his shoulder and one knee, he got the second body into position, arms and legs dangling.

For a moment Warrener hung there himself, breathing heavily, his arms draped across the body on the horse, sweat pouring down his face. Then he cleared his throat, straightened up and went back to leave the house as it would have been if two men had left it for good.

When he rode out, once more draped in the black

folds of the duster and with the two gruesomely laden horses on lead ropes behind his own blue roan, he took with him the Fords' ancient shotgun wedged under Dan'l Ford's body.

The way Warrener had it figured, once the Fords had sold to Logan they'd have moved out at once and headed for one of Wyoming's bigger towns. Casper on the Platte River away to the north east seemed to fit the bill. To get started for Casper it was necessary to cross Alan Forsyth's A Bar F ranch, which fitted in with Warrener's plans for creating a plausible story. That was the direction he took. By leading the horses low down along Lost Creek, he was able to keep his head off the skyline – though at that time of night who the hell would be about?

After a mile he grew weary of the game, moved away from the river and pulled the grisly caravan to a halt. Swung down. Dragged both bodies unceremoniously off the horses. He let them flop heavily into the dust, and dropped the shotgun on Dan'l's chest. The animals were skittish, the whites of their eyes showing. They could smell blood, and death. Warrener led them away so that they were some fifty yards north of where the bodies were dumped. He left them quivering but somewhat calmer, then trekked back.

On the way he took out the thick envelope, removed the banknotes and stuffed them into the pocket of his duster.

When he got to the bodies he tore the envelope so that it looked as if it had been ripped open in haste, crumpled it in his big fist then wedged it in the dust under Dan'l Ford's bony hip. He squinted away into the moonlight. The two horses were where he'd left them. Watching him. Ears pricked.

He grinned. If they were listening, hell, why disappoint them? He bent over Dan'l and picked up the shotgun, cocked it, pointed it at the clear skies and fired both barrels. The flash was dazzling, the blast stunning. Then he threw the shotgun down so that it lay close to Gray Ford, the more powerful of the two brothers; the man who, if they'd been attacked, would have tried to put up a fight.

Fifty yards away, the two horses had bolted at the roar of the big scattergun. They headed north at a wild gallop. If they kept going at that lick, Warrener figured, they should make it all the way to Alan Forsyth's ranch house. From those frightened horses, the discharged shotgun, the dead bodies of Dan'l and Gray Ford and the torn and empty Bald Hills' Bank envelope, it would be a simple matter for the rancher and his men to work out what had happened.

Even if the conclusion they reached was entirely wrong.

Maybe, Warrener thought, as he swung into the saddle and turned back down Lost Creek, he should follow the lead of Ned Buntline and make a career writing those dime novels.

TWELVE

It had been an easy matter to ride into Bald Hills in the heat of the day as a dusty stranger, just another rider passing through a busy small town. But, as Red Cavanagh had already discovered, it was something else again to walk into an establishment and meet face to face a man who, four years ago, had mourned your early death.

The coarse cotton shirt was chafing his horse-whipped back hard enough to put a permanent furrow in his brow, so Red at least had the excuse of being distracted when he rode into Bald Hills, tied his horse and walked into the bank. Morris Clark, too, was not paying much attention when Red appeared at the counter. The bank's owner was filling in for a clerk who had called in sick. He looked up, smiled and waited. When Red said that he wanted to make a deposit, Clark slid forward a pad of paying-in slips, held his pen poised and . . . well, took a longer look and went chalk white.

'Jesus Christ,' he said. 'Red? Red Cavanagh?'

Red smiled and nodded. He pushed a thick wad of

banknotes across the counter.

'I'm not too conversant with paperwork, Mr Clark, so if you could do the filling in and I'll sign on the dotted line.'

Clark was staring at him, stunned.

'I. . . .'

'Yeah,' Red said. 'Most people did.'

'But. . . .'

Someone behind Red coughed impatiently.

'Give me the blank sheet,' Red said, 'I'll sign then get out of here, trust you to do the rest.'

Clark nodded. He slid the pad forward, dipped a pen, watched Red take it. Looked hard at the banknotes, then up at Red.

As he reached across and pulled the money towards him he said, 'You've . . . done well for yourself.'

'For a dead man.'

Clark's eyes widened. 'Goodness, no, what I meant was there seems to be a considerable sum here.'

'There is.' Red signed with a flourish, and was unable to keep the amusement from his gaze as he met the other man's eyes. 'Just be thankful it wasn't your bank I robbed.'

Clark's mouth fell open. Red turned and walked out. His words had been overheard by other customers. It was like walking away from a packed church as the organ notes fade into silence.

His horse was already half asleep. With his back as painful as it was, Red mused, swinging into the saddle would be more trouble than it was worth. Why disturb both horse and rider? Besides, how far was he going? He turned and started down the plank walk. A short way down from the bank he passed Barney Malone's saloon. A swamper was splashing soapy water and whistling through his teeth. Across the street – hell, Red could hardly believe it – old Denny Coburn, unchanged after all those years, was standing in the doorway of his livery barn. That barn, Red recalled with the faint stirrings of anger, was now owned by Grant Logan.

He was about to stroll across and chat to the old hostler – either frighten him to death or bring unexpected delight his day – when he heard his name called.

John Vernon was jogging across the street from the café, slapping his hand on the tailgate of a trundling wagon, nodding his head to a rider. He stepped awkwardly up on to the plank walk and looked keenly at Red.

'You're moving remarkably freely.'

'I've you to thank for that.'

Vernon nodded, not really listening. 'I'm heading down to the council offices. Something's come up, a couple of deaths, and some movement on the local property market. You should come with me.'

'I was figuring on moseying on to the jail and having a quiet word with Flatfoot.'

'Quiet?' Vernon lifted a sceptical eyebrow. 'Sounds ominous but, don't worry, Jones will be one of those present.'

And, without waiting for a reply, the gunsmith was off down the street.

'Who else?' Red said, catching up.

'Officials. The usual. Wait and see.'

They hurried on in silence, the lame gunsmith sprightly and surprisingly difficult to keep pace with. The council held its meetings, Red remembered, in a couple of big rooms above the offices of the *Bald Hills Sentinel.* Exterior stairs led up the side of the newspaper building. Vernon went up like a mountain goat, and banged into the room without knocking.

Red followed more slowly. If Flatfoot was present, then other men there would, by now, know that Red was back from the grave. Nevertheless, his appearance there with Vernon would be unexpected. Though he had no idea what he was going to say or do, he thought surprise might be to his advantage.

When he walked in he found himself in a spacious room where the bright morning sun slanting through the window over the street turned smoke from cigarettes and cigars into a light, floating mist. Vernon had veered to one side, and was trying to open the window. Red saw big Lewis Edgar standing alongside a table, chin jutting as he looked towards the door, his jacket pushed back and his fists on his hips. Alan Forsyth of the A Bar F ranch was sitting at the table, looking much older than Red remembered. Off to one side, standing with one elbow hooked across the top of a battered green filing cabinet was the tall figure of Bald Hills' town marshal, Flatfoot Jones.

Temporarily disorientated by the dazzling sun flooding into the room, the thin floating haze of smoke and the strangely menacing presence of big men standing too close to him, Red had the sudden choking sensation

97

of being back in a sun-baked clearing with a hangman's noose beginning to stretch his neck.

The snapping blow to the jaw sent Flatfoot banging back against the wall alongside the filing cabinet. A faded tintype of dark-suited men with moustaches fell to the floor, shattered glass tinkling. The cigarette flew out of Flatfoot's mouth, and suddenly his teeth and lips were red with blood. Eyes wide with shock, he tried to raise his arms to protect his face as Red stepped in close. It was the wrong move. The next punch drove deep in under his ribs and breath hissed through his nose, spattering blood. He began to go down, doubled over. Again his hands dropped. Red's swinging elbow came over the top, caught him high on the cheekbone and knocked him sideways to the floor.

Then Lewis Edgar was behind Red, muscular arms wrapped tight around his body. As Red began to struggle, Edgar lifted him off his feet, wrestled him away from the filing cabinet and the groaning marshal and dumped him hard into a chair by the table.

'What in the name of God,' Edgar gritted, 'was all that about?'

'Should be easy enough to work out, Lew,' John Vernon said. 'Don't you remember, more'n four years ago, that crazy story told to us by Joe Parody and Flatfoot? If Red's here, as large as life, doesn't that tell you someone was lying?'

'I told the truth,' Flatfoot said. He spat blood on the boards, struggled to his haunches then sagged back against the wall. 'When me and Joe left that clearing,

Red was swinging at the end of a rope.'

'All you missed out,' Red said, fighting to keep calm, 'was who put me there, and who saved my life. Well, I'll save your breath, fill that bit in for you.' He looked across at Edgar. 'The rope was put round my neck by Joe Parody and Flatfoot Jones. The men who cut me down before I choked to death were the Willis Walton boys.'

'Why stop a good story there?' Flatfoot said, rolling awkwardly sideways and climbing up off the floor. 'Tell these fellows what you've been doing for the past four years—'

'That's diverting attention from your own crime,' Edgar cut in bluntly.

'What crime? The man who was supposed to have hanged is standing here in front of you.' Flatfoot shook his head. 'OK, so I did wrong then, but I've made up for it tenfold by my services to Bald Hills as town marshal. Four years, upholding the law.' He looked across at Red. 'Can Cavanagh say the same? Sounds to me like he rode out of that clearing with a bunch of no-good bank robbers. So what happened next?'

'I drifted,' Red said. 'Picked up range work when I could—'

'Bullshit,' Flatfoot said. 'For a coupla months you rode with what was left of the Willis Walton gang – hell, after Boulder City there was only Cole Willis, wasn't there? So it was him you rode with, but something went badly wrong and you ended up in a Texas jail. That's where you spent the last four years. Funny thing is, the money you made in that twelve months ain't never been recovered.'

'How do you know this?' Edgar said.

'Lawmen get dodgers, circulars. Bits of news that don't hit the papers gets passed around offices.'

'You been keeping this under your hat for four years?' Vernon said.

Flatfoot shook his head. 'No, nowhere near that long. All I got was notification of his release, and that was no more than a month or so ago. The rest came from a later piece written by a journalist on how much time Red had done, and the nature of his crimes.' He shrugged, dabbed at his mouth with his bandanna. 'That's how I found out he was alive, but I was surprised as anyone when I saw him ride into town.'

'This is all very entertaining,' Alan Forsyth said, leaning forward and speaking for the first time, 'and it's a pleasure to have this young man back amongst us, but I'm afraid we're getting bogged down in history.'

'Damn right,' Lewis Edgar growled, 'and none of it can be changed. Jones, go visit the doc, get that damaged mouth seen to. Red, I echo Alan's words most heartily, but right now you'd best go—'

'Red stays,' John Vernon said.

'Why?'

'Because,' Vernon said, 'the man who's sure to figure prominently in what we're about to discuss here is one of the reasons Red Cavanagh returned to Bald Hills.'

THIRTEEN

A patch of blood on the bare boards was all that remained of Flatfoot Jones. Lewis Edgar had lit another cigar, and continued pacing. John Vernon was at the table with Alan Forsyth, and Red Cavanagh had replaced him at the window. The sun was hot on his damaged back, his eyes hooded as he soaked up the comfort and listened to the A Bar F rancher.

'We all know that man is Grant Logan,' Forsyth said. 'His drive to take over a whole swathe of southern Wyoming has been the talk of the town for months. Last night he took another big step towards that goal by buying out the Ford brothers. Paid them in cash. Denny Hume called me into his office when I was passing, sat behind that big oak desk and showed me a crumpled bit of paper signed by Dan'l Ford.'

'A crude bill of sale. Is it legal?'

Forsyth nodded. 'Denny's a competent lawyer, Lew, so if he's satisfied then I guess Logan's got his hands on another patch of land.'

'And yet again it's to the north of town,' John Vernon

pointed out.

Red eased his position, stretched his back.

'Is that significant, John?'

'It's part of a pattern, but don't ask me what it means.'

'Yeah, well, that latest acquisition goes some way to confirming my suspicions,' Lewis Edgar growled. 'To put it bluntly, we've all been watching Logan with our eyes wide open but not doing any real looking; figuring he was just a rancher with big ideas without seeing what was right there in front of us. Well, I decided to do some digging, and ended up deeply shocked. And although Logan hasn't as yet done anything openly crooked—'

'I wouldn't be too sure of that,' Forsyth said. 'The Logans' saddled horses trotted into my yard early this morning. We found Dan'l and Gray a way down the creek. Both dead from gunshot wounds. Gray's shotgun had been discharged. It looks like they'd put up a fight.'

He reached into his pocket, pulled out a crumpled bit of paper and dropped it on the table. 'Found that under Dan'l's body.'

Edgar stepped across, poked it with a finger. 'Bank envelope. If their money was in that. . . .'

'For sure it was,' Forsyth said, 'and now it's gone. They were gunned down, then robbed. What troubles me is who the hell knew they'd sold up, knew they'd headed north and moved fast to relieve them of their cash?'

'If the sale went through late, the only person who could know is the man who gave 'em that envelope,' Red Cavanagh said, 'and that would be Grant Logan.'

Forsyth nodded. 'My first thought. And you're right, the deal must have been done late last night. I spoke to Morris Clark at the bank. Logan drew that cash out yesterday afternoon.'

'Couldn't have been Logan,' Vernon said. 'I watched him leave town on the Laramie stage.'

Forsyth was surprised, but unfazed. 'Then his son, Rick, would have completed the sale for him. Like father, like son.'

'No.' Vernon shook his head. 'Rick came to see me yesterday after Grant took a horsewhip to Red. He was angry and upset. Last night he stayed in a room over Barney's saloon. I don't think father and son have spoken.'

'Then it had to be that fancy gunslinger, Chet Warrener,' Lewis Edgar said, 'and if that's so then I'd say we're getting close to what might have happened out there on your land, Alan.'

'It was certainly Warrener who rode in early this morning and handed that bill of sale to Hume.'

'This is my third day back in Bald Hills,' Red said, 'and if there's one name I've heard mentioned almost as much as Grant Logan's it's Chet Warrener's. Popular opinion is that he's a gunslinger, an enforcer, a man brought in to push through Logan's dirty work. Yet the first time I saw him, he seemed to be having a heart-to-heart with the town marshal, Flatfoot Jones.'

Edgar nodded. 'It didn't go unnoticed. I asked Flatfoot what was going on. He told me gaining the confidence of undesirable characters gives him an edge if there's any trouble.'

'Can't argue with that,' Vernon said, 'as long as our marshal shares what knowledge he gains. Has he passed anything on? Do we know any more about Warrener now than we did on the day he rode in?'

Edgar shook his head. 'Nope. Grey hair and a certain world weariness puts him anywhere between forty and sixty. Looks hard as nails, damn near preens if he feels he's being watched. Hell, he's so full of himself he's got his initials carved on his gun butt, burned into his holster—'

'Chet Warrener,' Red cut in, and he rolled his eyes heavenwards. 'Initials CW.'

Edgar stared. 'So?'

'What did Flatfoot tell you not half an hour ago? Who did I ride with for twelve months?'

'Cole Willis,' John Vernon said, and grimaced. 'Same initials.'

'Same man,' Red said. 'He was always known for displaying his initials like some goddamn badge of honour. Every lawman had that detail down on their records. And that's another thing Flatfoot told you. Lawmen get dodgers, circulars. If that's how Flatfoot knows so much about me, he has to know all about Cole Willis, and must know the real identity of the man he's been talking to.'

For a few moments there was a thoughtful silence. Red knew the other men in the room, councillors all, were concerned about Flatfoot's deviousness but more intent on looking at Grant Logan's activities and his hiring of Cole Willis in terms of how it affected their town. For Red, it had become much more personal.

After years in prison he had returned to Bald Hills for several reasons, his childhood sweetheart Beth Logan being right up there at the top. Then, no sooner had he dumped his prison duds and set off on the ride north, rumours of trouble in the Wyoming town had aroused his interest and urged him to greater speed. After years of inactivity he was looking for excitement, even spoiling for a fight, but never in his wildest dreams had he expected to come across the old enemy, the man who had done so much to ruin a large part of his life.

John Vernon was watching him.

'If the man we now know is Cole Willis began fearing for his life when he heard you were in town—'

'Leave that between Red and Willis, let them sort out their differences,' Lewis Edgar cut in bluntly. 'Right now you need to know what's driving Grant Logan.'

'I think I know where this is leading,' Alan Forsyth said. 'What Logan's doing has to be for financial gain. As a businessman, that interests me, so I too have been doing some digging.'

'Go on.'

'I'll say three things: iron rails; Promontory; Utah.'

'You've got it,' Edgar said. 'It's still some years away, but what this country needs, and fast, is a transcontinental railway. The Central Pacific and Union Pacific will link. Promontory has been pencilled in as the place it's going to happen. But before the two grinning drivers shake hands in Utah, the Union Pacific has to cross southern Wyoming.'

'I couldn't get hold of details,' Forsyth said, 'possibly because they haven't yet been worked out, more likely because they're restricted. But even a simpleton will have realized that the government or the train operators will have to pay huge sums of money for the land they need.'

'And that any small, lazy settlement standing on the route the railroad takes could almost overnight become a boom town,' John Vernon said.

Forsyth nodded. 'Grant Logan has long been aware of that – presumably because he knows the right people. That's why he's been buying up businesses in town, and forcing small land owners to sell. And that's why he is never, ever going to get his hands on the A Bar F. He can be his most persuasive, sweet-talk me from here to breakfast time and, if that doesn't work, threaten me with his hired gunslinger – but I will not sell the A Bar F to Grant Logan.'

FOURTEEN

When the meeting finally broke up, it was well after midday. The town was busy, plank walks crowded, dust hanging in the hot air. Flatfoot was standing outside the jail talking animatedly to one of his deputies. He looked across the street and grinned at Red – or so Red thought. Then he realized that what he'd seen as teeth bared in a grudging smile was sunlight catching the white cotton wadding that the doc had packed into Flatfoot's damaged, bloody mouth.

A smile, Red thought philosophically, would have been out of place. He'd not only broken the skinny fellow's teeth, he'd also goaded him into letting slip information that could lose him his job. The circulars he received regularly as a town marshal must have given him Chet Warrener's true identity and, even as Red turned to head up the street towards Barney Malone's Blackjack saloon, he saw Councillor Lewis Egan striding purposefully towards the jail.

John Vernon had gone on ahead. He stopped outside his shop, and shouted back to Red.

'Ellie's in my rooms. Call in later, we'll all talk.'

Red lifted a hand in acknowledgement, heard the door bang, then strolled on by and walked the fifty yards or so that led him into the cool dimness of the saloon. He stopped just inside the door. It was, he realized, his first time in the place. He'd been seventeen years old when he rode out after the Willis Walton gang. If his pa had ever caught him in the Blackjack he'd have taken his belt to him.

The place was almost empty. He strolled towards the bar, spurs jingling, hearing the swish of sawdust brushing his boots, the clink of glasses, the low murmur of conversation from a couple of cattlemen he knew would be discussing everything from the robbery and killing of the Ford brothers to the going rate for Aberdeen Angus bulls.

Then he slowed, his eyes narrowing.

Cole Willis, the tall bank robber he knew so well, was leaning on the bar watching his approach. His eyes and the crooked smile were mocking Red, but every line of the man's sinewy frame suggested wariness, and the readiness to spring into explosive action.

The saloonist was Barney Malone, a fat man with several chins and a pink scalp bearing a finger of greasy black hair. He was a cheerful character, and nobody's fool. The sudden tension that crackled between the man he watched crossing the open floor, and Cole Willis, sent his hand probing beneath the bar. It came up clutching a hunk of thick wood, polished from frequent use, which he placed carefully within easy reach. Then he stepped back, folded his arms, and waited.

'Red Cavanagh,' Willis said softly, and Red saw Barney Malone's eyes widen slightly, his gaze fix on Red with sudden recognition. The saloonist let a smile flicker across his face, there, then gone. An almost imperceptible dip of his head let Red know that, while Malone might not side with him, he was prepared to see fair play.

'Ain't you too young to drink hard liquor?' Willis said, glancing sideways and winking at Malone. Then he grinned. 'Hell, I forgot. You've had four years doing hard time to do some growing up. Tell me, what's it like settin' all that time in a stinking cell looking at clear blue skies through iron bars?'

Without thought, Red stepped in close and ripped a punch up from somewhere around his right knee. There was the sickening crack of bone on bone as it connected with Willis's jaw and knocked him backwards across the bar. Barney Malone grabbed for the wooden baulk, scooped it out of reach. Dimly, Red heard chairs scraping, the hoarse curses as the cattlemen scrambled out of the possible line of fire, another drinker made a run for the street door. But his whole attention was concentrated on the bank robber. The man whose jaw had felt like a solid wall of stone was no Flatfoot Jones. He was far from finished.

For a moment Willis hung there, his body bent back at a painful angle. Then he used his own weight and a swing of his long legs to bring him off the bar. Both booted feet slammed down on the packed earth. Without a sound he charged at Red, swinging with both fists. There was a lot of weight packed into his lean frame. One blow looped high, crunched against Red's ear and set his head ringing. A second drove in low and hard, below his belt buckle. Pain knifed through his groin. He grunted, tried to cover up, but a third blow slammed him back against a table.

The flimsy wooden table slid across the floor. One leg snapped. Off balance, with no support, Red flapped his arms wildly. His clenched fist caught a chair, sending it skidding across the sawdust as he crashed down on his back. At once his lips pulled back from his teeth in a grimace of pure agony. Willis stepped forward, grinning. His clear intention was to leap high and drop down with both high heels, cracking Red's ribs.

'No, don't do it.'

The stentorian roar came from behind the bar.

Willis pulled back. He looked across at Malone and shrugged his shoulders. Then, as Red rolled sideways and came up on to his knees, the bank robber bent forward, clamped both hands on Red's collar and ripped the shirt from his back.

'Yeah,' Willis said, gloating, 'Logan told me how he'd been playing around with raw meat.'

And as quick as a flash he twisted the remnants of the shirt into a rope and lashed it across the scarred flesh, once, then again, a swift backhand stroke using a snap of the wrist.

A groan of agony was forced through Red's clenched teeth. He dropped flat, felt the swish of cold air as another stroke from the twisted shirt narrowly missed. Then, aware that in his weakened condition he'd bitten off more than he could chew, he rolled on to his back, the sawdust biting into his wounds, clinging to the fresh blood. He squinted up at Willis through streaming eyes screwed up against the pain that stretched from his neck to his waist.

'Instead of whipping a man when he's down,' another voice cut in, 'try facing someone fit enough to fight back and angry enough to plug you where you stand.'

'With a gun in your hand, cocked and pointing in my general direction,' Willis said, casting a glance towards the door, 'you sure have the edge over a man holding a piece of twisted shirt.'

John Vernon nodded. His face was grim as he came into the saloon, the sun throwing his shadow long across the sawdust, his eyes ablaze with fury.

'You OK, Red?'

Red climbed to his feet, rocked, stepped unsteadily away from the upturned, broken-legged table to lean an elbow on the bar.

'A bruised knuckle, a back as raw as fresh steak – yeah, I'll live.'

'To fight another day,' Willis said. He'd backed off, positioned himself so that if necessary he could throw down fast on Malone, Red or John Vernon. 'Isn't that what we always said, over the first drink, when we'd come through a scrape and rode clear of another mean town?'

'Those days are gone. The four hard years I've spent growing up gave me time to think, learn some sense.'

'But not enough to stop you poking your nose into trouble.'

'The same applies to you, because there's no sense in what you're doing,' John Vernon said. 'Last night you shot dead two harmless old men so Grant Logan could take over a few acres of scrub. That was cold-blooded murder. Then you pocketed the cash intended for those old-timers – and that's robbery.'

'If there was any proof I'd done those things,' Cole Willis said, 'Flatfoot Jones would have me in a strap-steel cell; the carpenters would be erecting the gallows.' He tossed the twisted remnants of shirt at Red. 'What happened last night was a legitimate cash purchase, and it puts Logan in a good position to buy the adjoining land and extend his holdings away to the north.'

'Alan Forsyth's A Bar F?' Vernon grinned, slipped his six-gun into its holster, rubbed his hands on his pants. 'It may be a little late in the day, but town officials have finally caught on to Logan's game. Well, he can forget it. I spent some time with Forsyth this morning, and I can tell you now, Logan hasn't a hope in hell of buying that spread.'

'He'll sell—'

'Get out of town, Willis,' Vernon said, turning away from the outlaw in disgust. 'The game's up, Logan is finished—'

'No, it's Alan Forsyth who's finished,' Cole Willis said.

'Forsyth—'

'Mark my words,' Willis said, the smile on his face cruel, his eyes the eyes of a devil. 'When Grant Logan gets back to town, Alan Forsyth will be hammering on his door begging the man to buy the A Bar F.'

FIFTEEN

It was, Red Cavanagh mused, an impressive start to what John Vernon had said was a noble cause. He'd been back in his home town no more than a couple of days and in that time he'd seen his childhood sweetheart snatched from under his nose, been horsewhipped for a sin he hadn't committed and lost a fist fight to a man he'd believed was more than a thousand miles away in southern Texas.

So far, the noble cause was going nowhere. He'd been too busy trying to stay alive to do anything to halt Grant Logan's drive to power.

'I had a quick word with Barney before we left the Blackjack,' John Vernon said. 'He told me you lashed out at Willis with little provocation. Care to tell me what that was about?'

Red was wearing one of Vernon's shirts, and once again drinking his fine whiskey in the rooms above the gunsmith's shop. Ellie Forsyth, a beauty in her early forties, was sitting opposite him. The flaxen hair he remembered so well was unchanged, and if the damage done to her spine when she fell from her horse had affected the muscles of her legs, nothing could be seen. She wore a long skirt, above that a soft white blouse, and her eyes were watching the gunsmith with intense interest.

'I can do more than that,' Red said, easing his back in the deep, comfortable chair. 'Seems like a good time to set the record straight, and the best place to start is four years ago.'

'The day you walked into my shop,' Vernon said, 'and asked for a rifle.'

'Yes. In the course of which discussion I told you the Willis Walton gang had killed my pa.'

'But that wasn't true.'

'It was as good as.' Red sipped his whiskey, looked across the glass at Vernon. 'Louis Cavanagh had never been a part of the gang, but he had a half-brother – his ma, my grandma, had married twice. The son from that first marriage was my uncle, Dustin Walton – which tells you where the second half of the gang's name came from. When the three of 'em rode in that night, they told Pa they intended robbing the Bald Hills bank. He tried to talk them out of it, told Dustin, his half-brother, he was out of his mind. They laughed, rode off into the night and Pa went and got good and drunk out of sheer frustration.' Red shrugged.

'That's understandable,' Ellie said. 'Goodness me, not only did his half-brother stand a good chance of getting killed; if he was caught robbing a bank then Louis would have been right there in the middle, his name dragged in the mud.'

'Yes, it's beginning to make some kind of sense,' Vernon said. 'Louis fell when he was too drunk to stand, didn't he? Their visit had caused him to act that way, so in your young mind they'd killed him. And I can see now why Dustin Walton stayed behind in the clearing after he and his pards had saved you from hanging. You were his nephew. It was Parody and Flatfoot who'd put the rope around your neck. He'd watched them high-tail, guessed they'd be back and he was damn well going to make them pay for their wickedness.'

'And although after what they'd done for me I was in their debt,' Red went on, 'I was still blaming them for my pa's death. Like my uncle, I wanted them to pay, but to stay close I had to be part of what they were doing. You were right, I was there holding the horses outside the bank in Boulder City, and I did cut Vin Devlin's cinch, but what happened next told me something: I was sick to the stomach when I saw him gunned down.'

'The young man I knew,' Ellie said, 'would have been appalled if he knew he'd caused another man's death.'

'So is that what happened over Willis?' Vernon asked. 'You rode with him, watched him sleeping in the flickering light of countless camp-fires, but the urge to kill had gone. Is that why he's still alive?'

'Far as I can recall, the intention was still there,' Red said, 'if not the will. Trouble is, it didn't take Cole Willis long to work out what I'd done to Vin Devlin. Once he had that figured, he waited a while, then acted. We were camped outside Austin. Willis snuck into town, looking like an ordinary drifter. He told the marshal and his deputies where they could find a man involved with the

115

bank job in Boulder City, then disappeared.'

'That was cowardly,' Ellie said.

'Sure, but I saw it coming.' Red looked at Vernon. 'Remember Flatfoot mentioning that the money from the Boulder robbery was never recovered?'

'This is a small town, Red. Morris Clark had already quietly suggested to me that you'd deposited a considerable sum in his bank.'

'Yeah. That was it. I stashed it before I was arrested, marked the spot, dug it up on my release. Ill-gotten gains, but what the hell. . . .'

For a moment there was silence. Then Ellie said, 'I think it's safe to say you were wronged from the day your pa died. And the right thing for Willis to do if he knew you were blaming him for your father's death would have been to have it out with you. Set the record straight.'

'The only outcome would have been a gunfight. Maybe he didn't fancy his chances. Deep down, cold-blooded killers are usually cowards.'

'Anyhow, I can see why you tried to break his jaw,' Vernon said. 'But now it's four years on from that day. You had a lot of time to do some serious thinking, so what about the unknown fourth member of the gang? Did his name come to you during one of those tortured, sleepless nights? Or had you already got it from Willis before he sold you to the law?'

'No to both. I'm beginning to wonder if there ever was a fourth man.'

'Oh, there was. The Willis Walton boys took a break for five years. When they returned, it was clear there was a man missing.'

Red's grin was rueful. 'Three outlaws cut me down from a tall tree. A few hours later, in the woods around that clearing, Clark shot my uncle, Dustin Walton. That left two. In Boulder City I dumped Devlin in the dust, and he was shot by a local hero with a shotgun.'

'Leaving Indian Cole Willis.'

'One dangerous man,' Red said, 'and no fourth was ever mentioned.'

'I've removed Flatfoot Jones. Deputy Ed Sloane's acting marshal,' Lewis Edgar said. 'Ed's a good man, but the promotion won't be permanent. I can't see him dealing with these Ford killings.'

'Could be there are more immediate and pressing concerns,' Vernon said, and there was an edge to his voice that caught Edgar's attention.

In the gathering dusk Edgar, Vernon and Red Cavanagh were standing talking outside the jail. The street was quiet, the dust of the day settled. Oil lamps had been lit in those premises that were still open. Their warm glow softened the approaching night.

An hour earlier, Ellie had been kissed tenderly by John Vernon, helped into her top-buggy and had headed for home. Vernon and Red had returned to the Blackjack saloon, shared a drink with Barney Malone, and sat at a table, drinking and talking. Red had become withdrawn, thoughtful. After a while he'd said Willis's parting words could have but one meaning, and that he needed to talk to Lewis Edgar. He'd avoided Vernon's eyes. The gunsmith, deeply disturbed, had accompanied Red down to the jail.

'Where's Flatfoot?' Red said now.

'Rode out of town. I expected anger, but he seemed unconcerned.' Edgar paused, took out a cigar, then looked across at Vernon. 'Let's go inside, you can tell me about those pressing concerns over coffee.'

The jail office was warm. The acting marshal was nowhere to be seen. Edgar said he was out talking to those businessmen who were still around, letting them know of Flatfoot's removal from office. He crossed to the stove, poured coffee into three cups, handed them round and sat behind the desk.

'So. . . ?' he said. 'Who's going to do the talking?'

'Earlier today we were both in the saloon when Cole Willis made a startling announcement,' Vernon said. 'Red had been bested in a fist fight, so it's understandable that the implications of what Willis had said took some time sinking in. When it did, it seems it planted some nasty ideas in his head. He's said nothing more, so, like you, I'm waiting to hear what they are.'

Red slid back a chair, straddled it, fixed Vernon with his gaze. 'You'll recall that Willis told us Alan Forsyth will soon be begging Grant Logan to buy the A Bar F. That suggests Forsyth is going to be put under intolerable pressure.' He shrugged. 'When I finally got around to it, I asked myself, what does Forsyth value more than the ranch, more even than life itself?'

Vernon's face tightened.

'His daughter, Ellie,' Edgar said, without hesitation.

'Beth Logan has been living in my cabin. On my first night back we both spent the night there, she was in one

118

room, I was in another. Somehow, during the night, she was spirited away without me hearing a sound. I know of only one man who could do that.'

'Cole Willis,' Edgar said, nodding. 'Known as Indian. So . . . what are you suggesting? He's going to work the same trick with Ellie Forsyth, take her somewhere and hold her hostage to force her pa's hand?'

'I think that's the kind of trick Logan will pull, if he's getting desperate.'

'Why go to the bother of sending Willis into the house? Ellie's seen often enough in her top-buggy. Usually alone.'

'Taking her in broad daylight's a risk. Willis will want time to get clear with her.'

John Vernon cursed softly. 'For Christ's sake, Red, why didn't you speak sooner? Ellie was right here, in town – hell, she was with us, in the same damn room.'

'If my brain hadn't felt like something dipped in molasses, I'd have been quicker off the mark,' Red admitted. 'As it was, by the time I'd got around to working out what Willis was telling us, it was too late to stop Ellie leaving.'

'Never mind. The important thing now is that if you're even halfway right we've got to move fast and—'

'Warn Forsyth? Sure, that's what we'll do,' Red said, 'but there's another idea has been gnawing away at me that could further complicate matters.'

Vernon flashed him a glance. 'Got something to do with what we were discussing with Ellie?'

Red nodded. 'Four years ago, the Willis Walton gang robbed Clark's bank. By that time I was already down

119

the trail looking for them. In that bank raid, Clark's young son, Tom, was shot dead because he was on the spot, the only lawman in town. So, tell me, when Parody and Flatfoot set out to hunt me down, who's idea was it?'

'Flatfoot's,' Vernon said.

'In hindsight, would you say that could've been him doing his damnedest to help those bank robbers.'

Instead of answering Vernon nodded slowly, thoughtfully, and turned to Edgar.

'Before today, Flatfoot had been marshal for four years, Lew. But how long was it before that when you gave him the deputy's badge?'

'That's an easy one, because no deputy had served longer. It was five years.'

'So he got that job about the time the Willis Walton boys hung up their guns,' Red said. 'When I rode into town a couple of days ago, first thing I saw was Flatfoot Jones talking to the man you now know is Indian Cole Willis.'

'It seems pretty obvious, doesn't it?' Vernon said softly. 'Our honest and upright town marshal, Flatfoot Jones, was the fourth man in the infamous Willis Walton gang.'

'He refused to help them rob the bank here,' Red said. 'Instead, he agreed to get Joe Parody out of town on some crazy pretext so that—'

He broke off as the street door banged open. The tall, trail-dusty young cowboy who walked in took a quick look around, spotted Red and looked sheepish. He spread his hands as if expecting a tirade of abuse, and was prepared to admit it was justified. What he heard brought a look of surprise to his face.

'Rick,' Red said, 'I believe I've got you to thank for telling John Vernon I was in trouble?'

'That's decent of you,' Rick Logan said, 'but I blame myself for not doing a hell of a lot more. I should have got between you and Dad when he tied you to that pole, made it clear he was in the wrong.' Then he grinned his relief. 'But now you can thank me again. The word from Beth is she's staying put for the time being, but she wants you to know it's not forever.'

'I remember saying something similar,' Red said, 'and it turned out to be four years.' He cocked his head. 'How did Beth get a message to you? Aren't you staying in town?'

'I was, but Dad's away, so. . . .' Rick shrugged.

'This is all very friendly,' Lew Edgar cut in impatiently, 'but it's wasting time and there's a job needs doing, and doing fast. Rick, are you heading home now?'

'Yep, I've completed what business I had in town, and Beth's message has been delivered. It's time for me to go.'

'Then I want you to deliver another message. It concerns a young woman, and this one's life could be in danger. It means you riding an extra few miles, but I want you to push on to the A Bar F and warn Alan Forsyth. It's highly likely your pa intends to use his daughter Ellie to force him to sell up.'

Rick frowned. 'But Dad's out of town. Far as I know he's somewhere back East.'

'The man we're worried about is Cole Willis.'

121

'Who?'

'You know him as Chet Warrener.'

'Damn.' Rick shook his head. 'Never could take to that man – and you're saying he's one of the Willis Walton gang?'

'He is, was – but we'll worry about that later. Priority now is to get to Forsyth, pass on that warning.'

'You think this Willis is going to try to snatch Ellie?'

'I'm pretty sure he was the man who took Beth from my cabin,' Red said, 'ghosted in and out without me hearing a sound. If he can do it once, he can surely do it again.

'I'm on my way.'

With a look of pure determination on his lean face, the tall cowboy swung on his heel and left the office. Seconds later they all heard the rattle of hoofs, fading into the night.'

'Damn it,' John Vernon said, 'we should have told Rick of our suspicions about Flatfoot Jones. That man's as mean as a rattlesnake, as wily as a fox. If he's now riding with Willis, protecting Ellie Forsyth could prove difficult, if not impossible.'

SIXTEEN

'I hear a rider. A way off yet, but coming on steady.'

Flatfoot Jones stepped out of the woods to the south of the A Bar F where he and Cole Willis had been whiling away the hours by a smokeless camp-fire, and gazed down the trail. They were close to where the Ford brothers had been gunned down and robbed. From there the trail followed Lost Creek for most of the way into town, cutting through what had been the brothers' spread and the eastern edge of Grant Logan's much richer Slash L. The moon was hidden behind high, thin cloud, casting a luminous half-light over the landscape.

'Sharper ears than mine,' Willis said.

'I've got me a bad feeling here,' Flatfoot said. 'If Edgar or Vernon's been putting two alongside two and getting the right answer, this could be someone out to warn Forsyth.'

'Goddamn. So what do we do, shoot him down? A night like this, the sound of a gunshot will be heard in Colorado.'

'Why kill him? When I was kicked off the job, my

badge went with me.'

'So?'

'I'll take a short ride up the trail, come back down again and meet this fellow. He'll be someone I know. With luck, he won't know I'm out of a job, and I'll spin a yarn.'

Willis chuckled. 'You always were the smart member of the gang.'

Flatfoot crackled through the brush to where the three horses where tethered, swung into the saddle and set off towards the A Bar F. He rode for no more than a hundred yards in the general direction of the distant lights of the Forsyth ranch, then turned back. When he passed the campsite, the rider was already closing. Despite the absence of a bright moon, he was recognizable.

'Rick,' Flatfoot said, as they met and drew rein. 'What are you doing heading away from home at this time?'

'Lew Edgar's got it in his head that that fellow Willis is out to harm Ellie Forsyth. Wants me to warn Alan to be on the lookout.'

'What d'you think I've been doing?'

'Well—'

'Was I in the office when you spoke to Lew?'

Rick laughed. 'Hell, no, you're out here.'

'That's right, warning Alan Forsyth to look after his daughter.'

'You've done that? So why did Lew send me?'

Flatfoot sighed. 'Because I thought it so important I didn't wait to tell Lew where I was going. My fault entirely that you've had a wasted ride, but at least that gal's safe.'

'Amen to that,' Rick said, heeling his horse and swinging it around. 'Thanks, Flatfoot, you always were one of the best.'

'Young and gullible,' Willis said.

'Why should he disbelieve me?'

'I said you were smart, not honest.'

Flatfoot chuckled. 'Well, it was a lie, sure enough, but it got us out of trouble and now it's up to you. You reckon the time's right?'

'I'll ride as close as possible, go the rest of the way on foot. It'll take me a while. By then the whole household will be snoring.'

'All two of them.'

'Or maybe just the one. That'll tell me where Forsyth's sleeping. His daughter will be the quiet one, I'll go for the silent bedroom where a woman lies dreaming.'

'A dream that's about to become a nightmare. You know she can't walk too well?'

'Even if she could, I wouldn't let her. Only silent way to get her out of there is to carry her. Only way to do that, stop her screaming and scratching my eyes out, is to put her to sleep with a gentle tap while she's lying there in her bed.'

'But not too hard. We need her conscious so she can ride that horse we brought along.'

'Smart, a liar, and a gentleman,' Cole Willis said, heading for his horse. 'I took two dead men up this same trail last night, belly down over their horses. Ain't no damn reason at all why an unconscious woman can't travel in the same manner.'

Two hours after Rick Logan had left town, John Vernon, one foot planted on the Blackjack saloon's rail, could no longer stand the strain.

'We made a mistake,' he said. 'Hell, Rick's a young rancher, not a cold, ruthless gunman. We sent him out to warn Forsyth, but what if he runs smack into Cole Willis out there on the trail? You imagine for one minute Rick will get past him?'

'No reason for Willis to stop him,' Barney Malone said, scalp glistening in the lamplight behind the bar.

'Willis will stop anyone he thinks might get in his way.'

'Why should he think that of Rick? Before he decided to stop in town, Rick rode that trail most every day.'

'As far as the Slash L. Beyond that he crosses the Fords' spread and he's on A Bar F land—'

'Finish your drink,' Red Cavanagh said.

'Red, that's the woman I intend to marry.'

'You're taking your time over it.'

'Yes, maybe, but if you think I'm going to leave her—'

'I don't. Finish your drink, and we'll ride out.'

'Ed Sloane's the acting marshal—'

'For Christ's sake,' Red exploded, 'will you make up your mind? Sloane's no older than Rick. You think a badge makes him bulletproof?'

'No. You're right.' Vernon tossed back his drink, stepped away from the bar. 'It's just. . . .'

'That now the decision's made, you're dithering,

thinking maybe you're acting like an old woman.' Red grinned. 'Well, take it from me, you're acting like an old man. Come on, let me show you how us owlhoots handle these situations.'

Red's horse was outside the gunsmith's shop; Vernon's in the livery barn. Red rode across the street with him. They roused old Denny Coburn merely to let him know that nobody was stealing his charges, and within minutes they were pulling a cloud of dust after them as they hammered out of town.

The high cloud had broken and the moon was bright and clear. All the way across Slash L land the waters of Lost Creek were like a ribbon of silver across the landscape, guiding them to their destination. But of guidance neither man had any need. John Vernon knew the area like the back of his hand; Red had been born there and forgotten nothing during his years of absence.

So they pushed on without talk, without thought, each man concentrating on what lay ahead, on what they might find. Red knew that Vernon must be tormented by fear for the woman he cared for deeply. He imagined how he would feel if the woman in danger was the much younger Beth Logan, and the chill he felt caused him to glance across at the older man in sympathy.

Then they had crossed the Fords' scrap of neglected earth, hit the A Bar F and the widening slash of trail and could see ahead of a them a ranch house with its roof painted by the moon, its windows in darkness.

'What's that tell you?' John Vernon growled.

'Nothing's happened – or we're too late?'

'If we could answer that,' Red said, 'we wouldn't be here.'

'But we are, and so was Rick, and not too long ago at that. I'd expect Alan to be awake, some lights on.'

They slackened their speed as they drew near, pulling their horses back to an easy canter. With the intention of calming Vernon's obviously frayed nerves, Red reasoned out loud that a visit from Rick didn't have to spoil the Forsyths' night. They were probably sleeping peacefully in their beds, so riding in nice and easy was better than scaring them half to death.

'After Rick's warning, us hammering on the door at this time of night will do that anyway,' Vernon mumbled.

There was a hitch rail in front of the house. They crossed the moonlit yard, dismounted and tied their horses and Red let Vernon lead the way across the gallery to the door. Beneath it, a faint crack of yellow light was visible. Vernon had scarcely raised his hand to knock than the door opened with a click and a creak and Alan Forsyth was peering out at them. His grey hair was tousled. He'd pulled on a pair of pants, but was barefoot.

'What's going on?' he said, and yawned.

'Might ask you the same,' Vernon said. 'Rick Logan put the wind up you, ruin your sleep?'

'I thought I heard a noise a little earlier,' the rancher said, 'so I got up to investigate. Nothing was happening, so I made myself a drink and went back to bed. Nearly made it, too, then I heard your horses—' He broke off,

128

suddenly realizing what Vernon had said. 'Rick? How would he put the wind up me?'

'Well, I admit we're not sure about Cole Willis, but to be on the safe side we thought it best to warn you and as Rick was heading home—'

'But he hasn't been here.'

'Jesus,' Vernon said softly. Red touched his shoulder. The older man pulled away.

'Is Ellie all right?'

'Sure,' Forsyth said, 'she's fast asleep.'

'You're sure of that?'

There was a silence that seemed to drag on as Forsyth stared hard at his two visitors. Then he took a deep breath.

'Rick's not been here. I don't know what you believe Cole Willis is supposed to be planning, so why don't you come in and explain?'

The living room was dim and cool. A lamp was lit in the kitchen, but it was at the back of the house which explained why the light had not been visible. Red followed Vernon in, shut the door behind him. The gunsmith was itchy, unable to keep still.

'Go check on Ellie.'

'I told you, she went to bed hours—'

'Please, Alan. Just see if she's OK. Then we'll talk.'

Forsyth's jaw bunched. He shook his head, then crossed the big room and went out, padding on his bare feet. Red walked to the window, looked out at the moonlit yard.

'Someone's watching from the bunkhouse door. I can see the glow of his cigarette—'

'Shut up.'

Red turned. Vernon was standing with his arms folded. He looked at Red. His eyes were pools of horror. Then a door banged. He jumped visibly. There was the rapid slap of naked feet. Alan Forsyth burst back into the room.

'She's gone. Her bed's empty.'

His weather-beaten face was as white as his hair. His hands groped blindly. He sank into a chair. One hand came up, rubbed his chest. His face was twisted in pain.

'There's a smell in there, male, sweat – animal smell, more like, and you're saying it's that sonofabitch Willis?'

'Following Grant Logan's orders,' Red said, 'to force you to sell.'

'But how—?

'He moves with the stealth of an Indian,' Red said. 'In and out, you wouldn't hear a sound.'

'Ellie would have screamed—'

'Willis would have made sure she couldn't.'

John Vernon swore foully. 'So help me I'll kill the bastard, and that swine Logan when he gets back—'

He snapped the words out, left them unfinished, swung around and ran for the front door.

'I'll go with you—'

'No.' Red turned and waved Forsyth back as he struggled to get up. 'This has hit you too hard, leave it to us.'

He watched the distraught rancher sink back into the chair, then raced after Vernon. The gunsmith was already in the saddle. As he wheeled his horse away from the rail there was a shout from the bunkhouse.

'What the hell's going on.'

130

'See to your boss,' Red cried, flinging himself on to his horse. 'He's looking bad, heart trouble maybe so you could need the doc. . . .'

Then he'd raked his paint with his spurs and was thundering across the yard after Vernon who was already fifty yards ahead of him and riding like the wind.

SEVENTEEN

It was but a short ride to the Slash L. By the time they crossed the Fords' land, Red was up with Vernon, the wind hard in his face, the relentless drum of hoofbeats like a pulse pounding in his ears. A glance across at the gunsmith's face beneath the blown-back, flattened brim of his hat told him that shouted words of encouragement would not be welcome. Vernon's face was set, his jaw jutting, his sole concern urging more speed from his straining mount.

Riding on the edge of panic, Red thought – but who could blame the man? And at least the panic wasn't dulling his brain. The logical way to discover how things could have gone so badly wrong was to talk to Rick Logan, and that's where they were going. And Red could see only two possible answers to the question Vernon would put to the Slash L heir. Rick had either forgotten that he was supposed to deliver a warning – in which case he would be lashed by Vernon's fierce rage as brutally as Red had been lashed by the senior Logan's horse-whip – or something had cropped up which made the ride to the A Bar F a waste of time.

Of course, there was the third possibility. Vernon's fear, voiced in the saloon, had been that Rick might run into Cole Willis on the way to Forsyth's ranch. In Red's opinion, if that had happened then Rick Logan would not be at the Slash L. He'd be lying somewhere in the scrub, with a bullet through his heart.

Such morbid thoughts flew from his mind as Vernon once more inched ahead and they swung sharply into the Logan family's yard. Here there was no serene darkness, no stillness or silence in the lambent light of the moon. Instead, from every window in the low white ranch house warm lamplight spilled to form pools in the dust, and from the open door of the bunkhouse waves of laughter gusted on the cool night air.

'Card game,' Red said. 'The cowboys are playing poker.'

'And the house? Why are they awake?'

'Could you sleep with that row going on?'

Vernon grunted. Again there was a convenient hitch rail. They flung themselves from the saddle, and the lean gunsmith hit the ground running with his characteristic awkward gait. Red tied the horses, then followed. This time there was no need to hammer on the door. It opened even as they were both striding across the gallery, and the tall figure of Rick Logan stepped out to meet them.

One question answered, Red thought. He hadn't been stopped by Cole Willis.

Rick grinned, opened his mouth to speak but was beaten to the punch.

'Why the hell didn't you warn Forsyth?' John Vernon demanded.

'Didn't need to, John. I met Flatfoot; he was on his way back from seeing him.'

'Flatfoot?' So furious was Vernon that he spun in a full circle, then again faced Rick with his hands on his hips and his eyes blazing. 'Was he with Willis?'

'No, he wasn't.'

'Not that you could see, but that gunslinger was there somewhere, keeping out of sight. All Flatfoot's doing, I'd say. You weren't to know, but Flatfoot Jones has been thrown off the job by Lew Edgar. He's a crook. He robbed banks with the Lewis Walton gang, he's as thick as thieves' – Vernon laughed jerkily – 'with Cole Willis and he sure had you fooled.'

Red left them to it. Light was spilling out through the open door, and across the living room he could see Beth standing, watching. Her dark hair was loose. She was tall and slender, a warm robe over her nightgown. He went into the house, walked softly across animal-skin rugs, took both her hands in his.

'Ellie Forsyth is missing,' he said softly.

'Oh, my God.'

'Beth, this is the first time I've spoken to you since you were taken from my cabin. What happened that night?'

She shivered. 'I woke up suddenly, and Chet Warrener was in my room. He told me to get dressed, walk out of the house and ride away with him. He told me if I made the slightest sound, he would kill me.'

'Warrener's real name is Cole Willis. I'm pretty

certain he's behind Ellie's disappearance.'

'But if he's Willis, you know him. Goodness, you must do, Red, he was one of those men, those bank robbers—'

'Yes, he's a big part of my tainted past, and it concerns you. I couldn't come home to you because a calculated act of treachery by Cole Willis put me in one place for four long years.' He saw her eyes widen, understanding begin to dawn, and he smiled. 'We'll talk about that some other time, maybe one evening when we're married and sitting on our cabin's gallery watching the sun go down. But what's happening now is upsetting for you, because if Willis has taken Ellie, it's your dad's doing. Taking Ellie is his way of holding a loaded pistol to Alan Forsyth's head – so we need to know quickly where Willis has taken her.'

'But how can I possibly—'

'I don't know. I'm clutching at straws. But you've lived here all your life. I've been away too long, forgotten too much – couldn't possibly know as much as you do about the Slash L.'

'You think he'll be holding her somewhere close – perhaps on our land?'

'That's what he's suggesting, and I agree with him,' John Vernon said.

He and Rick had come in from the gallery. Rick was looking chastened, but his head was high and clearly he'd been sticking to his guns. Red knew Beth's brother had been unaware that Flatfoot had been kicked out of office, so there had been no reason for him to disbelieve the former town marshal.

'Willis will stay close,' Vernon said, 'because a long

ride would be too much for Ellie, and he'd have his hands full.'

'But knowing he could be close doesn't help us,' Red said.

'No.' Vernon shook his head in angry frustration. 'Hellfire, within a twenty mile radius there's any number of places he could hole up—'

'What about one of the line cabins?' Rick said. 'Wouldn't he want to be under cover?'

Vernon stared. 'They empty?'

'This time of year, yes, they are.'

'Dammit.' Vernon paced forward agitatedly, then back, threw a swift glance towards the window then swung to face Red. 'We've got to start somewhere, right? Better to have a faint hope than none at all, and looking at those cabins gives us that.'

'We can start with the nearest,' Red said, 'then work our way out.'

'I'll show you the way.'

Red shook his head at Rick. 'No, you stay here, look after Beth.'

'Surely Willis won't come here?' she said, pale-faced.

'No,' Red said, grinning encouragement, 'but you need protecting from those noisy cowboys out there.'

He grasped her shoulders with both hands as she managed a faint smile, kissed her cheek, then again followed Vernon, who was already limping out of the door.

Red knew he was right about knowing less than Beth about Slash L, but it seemed he was also way behind John Vernon in his knowledge of the area. Once they were mounted, the gunsmith swung out of the ranch yard and headed back the way they had come, Lost Creek glittering on their right. This time, however, he didn't ride as far as the land the Fords had occupied. Instead, after no more than half a mile he again swung left so that they were heading in a westerly direction across Slash L land. They continued on that line for perhaps fifteen minutes, slowing considerably for there was no trail to follow. In the fading moonlight the horses picked their way with care over rough open pasture. Red stayed some way back. So content was he to leave this part of the search to Vernon that he was taken by surprise when the gunsmith abruptly drew rein.

'Someone's there,' he said softly.

He was pointing at an angle to their right. Less than fifty yards away a cabin stood backed up against a low grassy ridge. From the chimney a thin plume of smoke was like a line painted across clear moonlit skies.

'No lights.'

'If they're asleep,' Vernon said grimly, 'so much the better – but I'm worried about Ellie. If Willis hears us coming, God knows what that man will do.'

'The last thing he'll do,' Red said, 'is harm his hostage.'

Vernon shot him a grateful look. 'Dammit, you're right. Ellie is Grant Logan's bargaining chip. Willis is forced to keep her alive.'

'On foot, then,' Red said, and slid from the saddle.

As they drew nearer, six-guns in their hands, boots whispering through the long grass, Red pointed.

'Just two horses. Surely if Flatfoot's with them. . . .'

'Two is what I'd expect,' Vernon said. 'Ellie's none

137

too good at riding nowadays, Willis would be forced to. . . .'

He trailed off, anger thickening his voice. Driven by those thoughts he limped his way ahead, somehow managing to move silently until he was within a few yards of the cabin's door. Red caught up, touched the gunsmith's shoulder.

'Knock first – or kick the damn door down?'

Vernon glanced sharply at him. His sudden grin told Red he appreciated the compassion behind the humour.

'If I kick with my good leg,' he said, 'I'll fall over. You do it.'

'And once we're in, you go straight for Ellie.'

With those terse words, Red stepped past him. He heard the oily click as the gunsmith cocked his six-gun. He did likewise. Took a deep breath.

The door was flimsy. Red lifted his right leg, drove it forward like a battering ram. The frame splintered. The door crashed open, split down the middle and fell apart. Then, as Red fought for balance, John Vernon shouldered him aside and charged into the single small room.

'Hold it there,' he roared. 'Make a move, and you're dead.'

The high moonlight seemed to be filtered through thin muslin, barely lighting the cabin's interior. Nerves taut as bowstrings, Red stepped in and moved fast to one side of the door. He saw a stove, shelves, floor strewn with a litter of clothing and saddles, a wooden cot in the shadows on each side of the cabin. On those beds legs and arms were thrashing as the shocked occupants fought to free themselves from blankets. Then they were kicked aside. One man stood up, buck naked, his pale skin and the whites of his eyes shining in the gloom. The other slid to the floor and sat, one arm raised as if to ward off bullets. He looked at Red, at John Vernon, at the cold steel of the cocked six-guns, and shook his head and spat sideways in disgust.

'Jesus Christ,' he said, 'if this is a sample of Western hospitality I think I'll head back East.'

'A couple of footloose drifters,' Vernon said bitterly, 'from east of the Mississippi.'

'Forget them. We ruined their sleep, but wasted our own precious time. So where to now?'

'I don't know. The next cabin's ten miles across country. Looking at them all until we hit pay dirt is what we set out to do, but somehow I see continuing as even more time wasted.'

They were back with their horses. Vernon was taking the weight off his leg, standing with an elbow resting on his saddle as he gazed into the distance. There was a haze around the moon. His breath was a faint white mist, like cigarette smoke, drifting on the first suggestions of a coming breeze.

'Any plan is better than none at all,' Red pointed out. 'Time spent standing still is time wasted in the worst possible way, and does Ellie no good – unless, while doing nothing, you can come up with a better idea.'

Vernon didn't answer at once. When he did, it was with a question.

'Do you know what that is over there?'

He was pointing to the north.

'If you mean what I think you mean,' Red said, 'I'd say it was a pretty ordinary stand of timber, stretching across country about a half mile away.'

'On whose land?'

'Tell me.'

'The Fords',' Vernon said, 'or it was.' Suddenly there was an undercurrent of excitement in his voice. 'The story goes that way back in the past an old trapper built himself a cabin. What with Indians and white renegades on the prowl in those pioneering days, he figured the safest place for it was in that stretch of woods.' Vernon turned to look at Red. 'The Fords took over that old trapper's cabin, lived in it for years.'

'Until last night,' Red said, suddenly seeing where Vernon was leading him. 'And last night they had a visitor. That visitor was Willis. He shot them dead, dumped the bodies on Forsyth's land.'

'Which leaves the cabin empty,' Vernon said.

'Dammit,' Red marvelled, 'I bet the idea of using it came to Willis even while he was lifting his six-gun to plug those old-timers.'

'I could be wrong.'

'Twice in one night?' Red grinned, then sobered as he looked again at the woods that were a low dark smudge against countless miles of open prairie. 'I'm pretty sure you're right this time, John, so how do you want to play it?'

'It's occurred to me,' Vernon said, 'that if they're holding Ellie there, Willis and Flatfoot could be sharing sentry duty. To be on the safe side.'

'That's a risk we'll have to take.'

'Could work in our favour. A man loses heart out on his own. If one of them is on watch, he'll be at the eastern edge of the woods. The trail from town runs alongside Lost Creek. They'll expect trouble to come from that direction.'

'Then what we do,' Red said, 'is play to their expectations. Also, we split up, but to our advantage. I ride in first.'

'Ellie's my concern.'

'We've already decided she's not in any danger. Besides, you care for that woman. If you see that he's hurt her you're liable to go off half-cocked. Me? Well, you heard Flatfoot shooting his mouth off. I'm a former bank robber with a grudge, an ex-con riding in to settle with the man who got me four years in a stinking Texas jail. And it doesn't matter who's out there smoking, yawning, trying to stay awake. When I ride in bold as brass, that's the sentry fully engaged. . . .'

Red's words trailed off. He stood for a moment, gnawing at his lip in thought. Then he nodded slowly. Watching him, Vernon grinned.

'I think you're thinking what I'm thinking.'

'What I'm *realizing* is the infernal din I intend making when engaging the sentry in mortal combat could create a handy diversion, draw whoever's in there with Ellie out of the cabin.'

'And that noisy diversion will prove invaluable if I'm in position close to the house. So I go in first, you wait, give me . . . well, whatever it takes.'

141

'You think you can do it? Ride along the north edge of the woods without raising the alarm, alerting the sentry or that feller in the cabin?'

'On foot, I'm a lame man pushing towards old age,' Vernon said. 'On horseback, I'll put Indian Cole Willis to shame along with the men in tepees who taught him his craft.'

EIGHTEEN

Looked at from the town trail alongside Lost Creek, the woods lying along the northern edge of what had been the Ford brothers' land had diminished to the single pointed section that was their eastern end. Somewhere in there, Red thought, I'll find Cole Willis or Flatfoot Jones. He couldn't see Willis putting himself to the discomfort of hunkering down in damp woodland for some of the coldest hours of the night. So it was odds on Flatfoot would be on watch, Willis with his boots up on the table in the cabin guarding Ellie Forsyth.

From the spot close to the line cabin where they had ground-tethered the horses they'd made their way back to the trail in a matter of minutes, then taken time to go over the plan – such as it was. Then they'd clasped hands, and Vernon had moved off in the moonlight. Now he'd been gone for an estimated five minutes. Because of the particular care he would be forced to take to avoid detection, they had agreed to give him a full quarter hour.

Red didn't have a pocket watch. Once he figured five

143

minutes had passed, he stopped counting. Then, when he judged that three times those five minutes had passed, he moved off.

Vernon had ridden wide to the north of the trees, exercising extreme caution. Red rode straight towards the woods, staying out in the open and putting his horse to a brisk canter. He was running a big risk by announcing his presence. The stakes were high. It was possible the man on guard wouldn't bother crying out a warning; that to avoid complications, any warning shot would be aimed to kill.

They were chilling thoughts. Plans were fine in the making, more nerve-racking in their execution. That particular thought had Red struggling not to laugh out loud, and he was level with the southern tip of the woods and still trying to keep a straight face when the warning came.

It was soft, menacing, from very close by.

'Don't come no further, Red.'

Flatfoot.

Red allowed a grin to surface.

'Hell, Flatfoot, it's not you I'm after. Where's that pardner of yours? Me and him, we have a score to settle, and there's no better time for it than right now.'

'Turn around, kid, go back to town. Better still, get the hell out of Wyoming.'

'You're mumbling, Flatfoot. Jaw still giving you trouble? Woes mount up, always come in a bunch. I guess you're blaming me for your sudden change in fortune.'

'Let's say it will give me great pleasure if I'm forced to

drill your miserable hide.'

Red clucked his disapproval.

'Nobody's forcing you to do anything, least of all hunker down in the woods on a miserable chill night.'

While talking he was holding his paint still and gazing into the dark timber to his right, waiting for night vision to come to his aid. He thought he saw a slight movement, a branch trembling; the glint of metal in the deep shadows. But that wasn't sufficient. Flatfoot could see him clearly, which put Red at a clear disadvantage.

So. . . . When the odds are stacked against a man, he must fall back on guile and animal cunning. Weigh up the situation. Figure out the best way of discombobulating the opponent. Then act accordingly.

There was no reason for Flatfoot to believe Red had anybody with him. Red was exposed. The ex-marshal was in deep shadow within the woods, had the drop on him and was probably crouching behind one of the bigger trees, which would shield him from flying lead. Common sense would tell him Red would realize a wrong move would probably be his last. He would expect him to back off.

Play to their expectations.

Muttering under his breath, Red clicked his tongue to his horse and began turning as if he was about to leave. As he did so, with his left side facing Flatfoot's position, his right hand dipped to draw his six-gun. His body masked the move. He rode ten yards. That took him clear of the end of the woods. Then he spurred hard left to put some timber between him and Flatfoot – but not too much. Pulling his horse to a halt he turned in the saddle and fired three spaced shots. The first two snicked wickedly into the woods, slicing towards the hidden man. The third split the air as Red pointed the six-gun at the sky. Three shots fired in that manner, he figured, was a recognized distress signal. Cole Willis would burst from the cabin and come running. Maybe he'd pause to lock the door – maybe not. Didn't matter. The rest would be up to John Vernon.

As for the first two of those three shots, they sent a different signal to Flatfoot Jones. It was the last he'd ever hear. As the reverberations died away, Red heard a drawn-out, gasping moan. It was followed by the sound of undergrowth crackling, and silence.

Red waited, counted slowly to sixty.

Then he turned his horse, slid from the saddle. He left the reins trailing, ran lightly across grass that was wet with dew. When he reached the woods he stopped. Once again he counted to sixty, all the time listening. Then, holding the cocked six-gun in front of him, he took a step into darkness. A twig snapped underfoot, another, the sounds like distant gunfire. He closed his eyes, waited, breathed his relief: there was no reaction; no blast of gunfire; no blinding muzzle flash followed by the agony of a wound.

But, according to John Vernon, Flatfoot always was a crafty sonofabitch. Lying doggo? Playing possum? Or plugged plumb centre and lying flat on his back gazing sightlessly at the canopy of leaves?

One way to find out.

Four more stealthy steps, soundlessly brushing aside snagging branches, breathing softly through his open

146

mouth. At the fifth step, Red's foot snagged on something soft but solid. Hair prickling, he fell sideways and
cracked his shoulder and the back of his hand painfully
against rough bark. The pistol jerked loose, almost fell.
Like lightning he recovered, twisted and pointed the
six-gun at the ground. Heart pounding, he waited.
Crazily, he thought of counting to sixty yet again, and
yet again amusement brought him close to laughter. He
cursed himself for a fool, and went down on one knee.
When he stretched out his left hand he touched coarse
clothing covering a warm body, felt the sharp bones of a
thin man and the wet stickiness of fresh blood.

There was just enough light filtering through the
trees to show him the black stain on Flatfoot Jones's
white shirt, his pale face, his staring eyes.

Red stood up, flexed his shoulders, looked about him
and thought hard. Flatfoot was dead, the signal would
have been heard and Willis wouldn't hang about. But
would he come fast and hard, or slow and easy, hoping
to take a marauder by surprise?

Well, John Vernon had ridden along the northern
edge of the woods to hit the cabin from that side. Red
had ridden along the southern fringe to locate Flatfoot,
then fallen back to go into the timber from the Lost
Creek end – the eastern tip of the woods – after plug-
ging the ex-marshal. The direct way for Willis coming
from the cabin would be to ride deep in the shadows
along the southern fringe. But the direct way, as the
outlaw would know full well, would announce his
approach as surely the bugles signalling a cavalry
charge.

147

The thinking had taken Red no time at all – and neither had it Willis. Had some sixth sense told him that the man causing him trouble was Red Cavanagh? Had he figured correctly that one outlaw trying to sneak up on another wasn't going to work, that a game of cat and mouse was no way to get the job done? It seemed that he had, and had opted for boldness. For even as those thoughts crossed Red's mind, there came the drum of hoofs fast approaching and through the timber Red saw a horse and rider loom dark against the night skies.

Abruptly, the rider drew rein, spinning the horse to a halt so that it snorted and tossed its head, and kicked up clods of earth. He had spotted Red's horse where he had left it, ground tethered, its breath a white cloud on the night air.

'If that's you in there, Red,' Cole Willis called, 'I guess old Flatfoot's died with his boots on.'

'On their back in dark woods, or face down bleeding into the dust of a town square after another bank raid – didn't most associates of yours die hard?'

'Vin Devlin did, in Boulder city, thanks to you,' Willis said. 'Flatfoot, now, well, he might have died a rich man if he hadn't turned the Bald Hills' bank robbery down four years ago. You know we put it to him after we'd talked to your pa?'

Anger swelled within Red Cavanagh.

'I know if you hadn't visited my pa, he most likely would have died in contented old age.' He paused, swiftly calculating the odds, realized he had wasted time thinking: there was now no chance of his bursting from the woods without being gunned down. 'Maybe you didn't know it at the time, Cole, but that visit killed him. The least you can do now is face me man to man.'

'That's what I intend, if you're up to it.' Willis chuckled. 'Skulking there in the shadows, you set a man to thinking maybe your guts have leaked away, your backbone got stained a sick yellow.'

Setting his jaw, keeping a tight hold on his increasing anger, Red holstered his six-gun. Then he picked his way out of the undergrowth, thorns ripping his clothes. When he stepped into the moonlight, he was met by a chilling sight.

Cole Willis towered over him, a black figure mounted on an excitable horse he was trying hard to control. The gunman was draped from shoulders to ankles in a lightweight black duster coat. In the slight breeze its tails flapped like sinister pennants borne by an emissary of the Devil.

Two bold strides took Red from shadow to moonlight. Watching Willis's eyes gleam as he reined the skittish horse round to follow the movement, Red said, 'You still have the advantage.'

'Up here? Maybe, but this duster's a big handicap.'

'Shuck it – then step down.'

The black duster billowed. Red stepped back. What would Willis try? Turn the horse as if to dismount, then spur straight at Red, let the horse cut him to shreds with flashing hoofs? Cowardice took many forms, and with narrowed eyes Red watched the outlaw struggle with the flapping coat.

Then the horse seemed to go wild. Its head jerked.

Bared teeth and the bright steel of bit and bridle rings flashed in the moonlight. Rearing, straining to run but held back by reins like taut bowstrings, the horse snorted fiercely and worked its way side-on to Red.

And from under Willis's left arm a muzzle flash blazed like a fierce red eye and Red was slammed in the shoulder by a blow that knocked him off his feet.

Fooled, dammit! The horse had reacted to Willis's cruel use of a Mexican rowel. The gunman had ripped at the animal, forced it to rear in agony while he calmly drew his six-gun and slid it across his body. Indian Cole Willis was right, for that was an old Indian trick.

Bitter recriminations flashed through Red's brain as instinct jerked him into action. He rolled frantically towards cover, coming down hard on his injured shoulder. A bolt of agony shot clear to his fingers, but the move saved his life. A second bullet thumped into the earth by his head. A third snapped the heel from his boot. The fourth parted his hair like a woman's hot curling tongs – then he was back in the undergrowth. He wriggled on to his belly, squirmed under the barrier of thorns, fought his way to a tree and gasped breathlessly as he gained its far side and sat with his head back against the trunk.

And then, despite the agony, the hot feel of blood coursing down his arm to soak his sleeve, once again laughter threatened to bubble to the surface. Four long years it had been, and damned if he wasn't pinned down in the same situation he'd faced in the clearing when Flatfoot and Joe Parody had been chasing him with a hangman's rope.

Flatfoot Jones was there again, not a couple of yards in front of him – but this time he was stone cold dead.

NINETEEN

The creak of saddle leather told Red that Cole Willis was dismounting. Desperately he tried moving his left arm, gritted his teeth at the stabbing pain, felt physically sick as he was swept by a wave of dizziness. Sitting down, he felt dizzy. What did that say for his chances in a stand-up gunfight? If he got both feet under him and straightened up, he'd fall right down again. Try to flee for his life, he'd probably run into a tree. The alternative? Well, fighting from a sitting position was less effort – but surely he could come up with a better idea?

Red smiled grimly, racked his brains – to no avail. He kept his ears pricked for the sound of Willis entering the woods. With his good hand he lifted his pistol, checked the loads. As he did so, high clouds drifted across the moon. The shining tips of bullets became dull lead, the sheen faded from Louis Cavanagh's six-gun. Darkness fell like a thick blanket over the woods. It seemed as if even the silence intensified.

'You going to hide in there all night?'

'Feels like home. Mattress filled with straw. Dark.

Confined. Man outside on guard with a gun.' Red let that sink in. 'Why'd you do it, Cole?'

'You blamed us for your pa's death. You got Vin Devlin, there was just me left and I knew you aimed to kill me. Getting you locked up in a prison cell eased my mind considerable—'

Red flicked his hand backwards around the tree and snapped a wild shot.

In the gloom the flash was dazzling. Cole Willis laughed, fired twice. Accurately. Bark chips flew from the tree. Red waited for his vision to return – and the first thing that caught his attention was the body of Flatfoot Jones. Indistinct, deep in shadow – but the sight of the dead man was an inspiration.

Suddenly his mind was seething with ideas.

Flatfoot was lying tangled in grass and undergrowth so that most of his legs were hidden. He was on his back, wearing a soiled white shirt. Red's shirt was white, and far from clean. His vest was almost identical to Flatfoot's, the same drab style and colour as those worn by thousands of cowboys across the West. Their hats were different, but that was good. Flatfoot's was a grubby black. Red's was grey and distinctive; along with its broad band and plaited neck-cord it would be recognized by anyone who knew him. And how difficult was it to change hats with a dead man?

Willis was getting impatient. He shouted something Red couldn't make out, directed a shot into the woods but he was firing blind and the next went miles wide. Well, Red would change all that. He slipped the six-gun into its holster. Carefully, gingerly, he turned sideways so

153

he could get his knees under him, pulled himself to his feet with the aid of quivering muscles and a tree trunk. He stood leaning weakly, breathing deeply, settling his pounding heart. Then he let go of the tree, turned and took a shaky step towards Flatfoot.

Brush crackled underfoot.

The most he could see in the darkness was the patch of white shirt.

For the second time that night he kicked a body. This time, when he dropped to one knee, the body was cold. His left arm was useless. He reached across to pluck Flatfoot's hat from his head and throw it as far as he could through the trees. Then he fumbled with the cord at his throat, slipped off the grey hat and dropped it over Flatfoot's face.

He took Flatfoot's six-gun, checked the loads; it was full. Thrust it into his belt.

And that, Red figured grimly, was the easy bit.

Again he struggled to his feet. He took another couple of steps deeper into the woods, reached a stout tree, stepped behind it. And now it's two trees, he thought, and wondered if he should stretch out his arms for branches; wondered if he'd lost so much blood he was delirious. Laughter bubbled again. This time he let it rip. It was a release. It was also intended to further confuse the bank robber. His roars of mirth rang out through those dark woods – then, as quick as a flash, he choked off the laughter, drew his six-gun and began blazing away in the general direction of Cole Willis's position.

There were a few split seconds of hiatus, then the fire

was returned. And now Willis had a target. Instead of firing blind into dark woods he was guided by the muzzle flashes from Louis Cavanagh's six-gun. Exactly as Red had planned. Still firing, he turned sideways behind the tree, made himself as thin as he could. The noise was deafening. Bark was flying, hissing through the air. Gunsmoke drifted acridly on the faint breeze. Willis stopped firing – probably to reload. Then Red's pa's gun clicked on an empty chamber. Without hesitation he pouched it and resumed firing with Flatfoot's .44. He counted the shots, fired two, three – then Willis opened up again. Red waited, fired once more. Then, as Willis's six-gun cracked again, and yet again, Red let out a deep scream of intense agony.

He let it trail off, become a wailing moan. Stamped down hard with one foot, creating the kind of noise a heavy body might make falling into dense undergrowth. Then he grunted once – and went silent.

There was a breathless hush.

It lasted for several minutes. Red knew Willis was waiting, listening. He'd heard the sounds that suggested Red was mortally wounded, but wouldn't easily be fooled. So he'd try to wait out the other man, see whose nerves were the first to break. But that could go on for just so long. In the end, Willis would have to come into the woods and look for the body.

At last, as the chill night air began to penetrate Red's clothes and he started to shiver, he heard a muttered curse. A horse snorted softly. There was the faint jingle of a bridle as Willis trailed the reins. Then there came the whisper of boots in grass, and scrub crackled as

Willis pushed his way into the woods.

Red was secure behind his tree, but fast weakening from loss of blood. He slid down the tree on to his knees, rested his forehead against the bark and wondered if he could stay conscious. And if he could do that, if he'd then have sufficient strength to lift the six-gun.

Flatfoot Jones's body lay between him and the edge of the woods: six feet away, his white shirt bloody, Red's grey hat covering his face. The moon was still obscured by cloud. Under the canopy of trees it was as dark as the inside of a cave. Red's eyes still hadn't recovered fully from the blinding muzzle flashes. As far as sight was concerned, Willis would be in the same poor shape. Red heard him stumble, curse, swear again as thorns snagged his clothes – and then he tore his way through yet more scrub and he was there, big even without the black duster, looming over Flatfoot's body. He was there for an instant – then he was gone.

'Aargh, dammit to hell.'

He'd tripped, planted both hands on the cold corpse and a white shirt stiff with the stickiness of drying blood.

'Well, now, Red Cavanagh. . . .'

There was a gust of triumph in the man's voice as he saw the grey hat, but at the same time a tinge of doubt. He was still wary, still half-expecting a trap, but eager to believe Red was finished, dead. Red saw him lean forward, sweep the hat from the man's face, lean down close to study the features. Then he rocked back to sit on his heels, shaking his head.

It was too dark.

For a moment he was still. Then he snapped his fingers. His hand came up and he reached into a vest pocket. Something rattled; cardboard, thin wood. There was a snick as Willis used a thumbnail to ignite a lucifer. It flared into light, as bright as a flaming torch in those dark woods, and Cole Willis leaned forward and held the match cupped in his hand so that he could see the dead man's face.

Weakly, Red Cavanagh hoisted the six-gun, drew back the hammer and shot Cole Willis in the back.

TWENTY

It was two weeks later. Marshal Red Cavanagh was sitting behind his desk. A white cotton sling hung loose from his left shoulder, but he had his arm out and was rubbing it reflectively. The shoulder wound was almost healed. The main problem now was the itching.

His wife of seven days had just kissed him and walked out to join Ellie Forsyth in the top-buggy and head off for an afternoon at the A Bar F. Her chestnut pony was trotting behind the buggy on a trail rope. Red knew Beth would be back in the cabin cooking his dinner long before he got home, and a contented smile softened his face at the thought.

There was a rumble across the street, and the Laramie stage pulled in. Red rose from the desk and went to watch from the sunlit doorway. The dust cloud overtook the stationary stage and rolled on down the street. Passengers stepping down ducked their heads, or held kerchiefs to their mouths while hurrying off about their business.

One of those was Grant Logan. His face was like

thunder. He strode up the street to old Denny's livery barn to collect his horse. Five minutes later he rode out of town at a gallop.

A couple of hours after that, with the sun dropping in the west and shadows lengthening, Rick Logan rode into town. He pulled in at the jail office, tied up and stamped across the plank walk. He looked excited when he walked in.

'It's all fallen through.'

Red was again behind the desk, writing. 'What has?'

'Those purchases Pa's been making are never going to make him a fortune.'

'Because?'

'In a few years' time the rail's going through all right, but Pa got his figures wrong. The two lines'll join up at Promontory in Utah, sure, and the Union Pacific will cross southern Wyoming – but its route will be too far north of Bald Hills. Pa won't hear those trains whistling even if he climbs up on the roof of the house and cups his hand to his ear.'

'Well I'll be damned,' Red said softly.

Rick flapped some papers. 'I'm off to see Denny Hume. I've to hand him back the deeds to that Ford land, get him to sell it.'

Rick frowned. 'You know the cash for that sale was found on Willis? He robbed the Fords. If they never got the cash, isn't the land still theirs?'

Rick shrugged, grinned merrily. 'Let them sort it out. All I know is, from now on Pa will be doing a lot of selling, and there'll be a lot of happy faces in town.'

When he'd gone, Red sat back for a moment, thinking.

159

Then he reached for his grey hat, planted it on his head, let the plaited cord fall beneath his chin and walked to the door.

John Vernon and Ellie were also planning on getting married – it had almost been a double wedding. Trouble was, Vernon's rooms above the shop were too small for a couple, and they certainly weren't going to live on the ranch with Alan Forsyth. Now, if the Fords' land was available, and the old cabin in the woods was knocked down and rebuilt. . . .

Red stepped out on to the plank walk, lifted his face to the warm evening air, looked contemplatively up the street at Morris Clark's bank.

Of course, land and construction work required money. However, if Vernon and Ellie liked the bones of the idea when put to them, well, Red just happened to know where a lot of cash was sitting idle. And if, additionally, they didn't object to putting cash with that tainted provenance to good use, well. . . .

Whistling happily through his teeth, Red Cavanagh hitched up Louis Cavanagh's gunbelt and started up the street towards the gunsmith's shop.